A few thoughts from Familiar...

It looks as if Nicole is out for the night. I don't know why I never considered that she might have a boyfriend. That's the most likely explanation for the fact that here's her car and there's no sign of her in her trailer. I doubt she walked anywhere. This movie set is on the backside of nowhere. So she obviously caught a ride with someone.

Should I be worried? It just seems hard to really worry about Nicole. She's so physically competent.

And if I'm any judge at all, I think Jax McClure is equally impressed. I get the feeling that Jax is a man who doesn't believe he's vulnerable to a woman's charms. He's one of those tough guys who believes he's had his last romantic bronc ride. Well, I do believe he's getting ready to learn differently.

All I can say is, "Cowboy up!"

Dear Harlequin Intrigue Reader,

Beginning this October, Harlequin Intrigue has expanded its lineup to *six* books! Publishing two more titles each month enables us to bring you an extraordinary selection of breathtaking stories of romantic suspense filled with exciting editorial variety—and we encourage you to try all that we have to offer.

Stock up on catnip! Caroline Burnes brings back your favorite feline sleuth to beckon you into a new mystery in the popular series FEAR FAMILIAR. This four-legged detective sticks his whiskers into the mix to help clear a stunning stuntwoman's name in *Familiar Double*. Up next is Dani Sinclair's new HEARTSKEEP trilogy starting with *The Firstborn*—a darkly sensual gothic romance that revolves around a sinister suspense plot. To lighten things up, bestselling Harlequin American Romance author Judy Christenberry crosses her beloved BRIDES FOR BROTHERS series into Harlequin Intrigue with *Randall Renegade*—a riveting reunion romance that will keep you on the edge of your seat.

Keeping Baby Safe by Debra Webb could either passionately reunite a duty-bound COLBY AGENCY operative and his onetime lover—or tear them apart forever. Don't miss the continuation of this action-packed series. Then Amy J. Fetzer launches our BACHELORS AT LARGE promotion featuring fearless men in blue with *Under His Protection*. Finally, watch for *Dr. Bodyguard* by debut author Jessica Andersen. Will a hunky doctor help penetrate the emotional walls around a lady genius before a madman closes in?

Pick up all six for a complete reading experience you won't forget!

Enjoy,

Denise O'Sullivan
Senior Editor
Harlequin Intrigue

FAMILIAR DOUBLE

CAROLINE BURNES

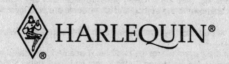

TORONTO • NEW YORK • LONDON
AMSTERDAM • PARIS • SYDNEY • HAMBURG
STOCKHOLM • ATHENS • TOKYO • MILAN • MADRID
PRAGUE • WARSAW • BUDAPEST • AUCKLAND

ISBN 0-373-22729-9

FAMILIAR DOUBLE

Visit us at www.eHarlequin.com

Printed in U.S.A.

ABOUT THE AUTHOR

Caroline Burnes has written seventeen books in her FEAR FAMILIAR series. She has her own black cat, Familiar's prototype, E. A. Poe, as well as Miss Vesta, Gumbo, Maggie and Chester. All are strays and all have brought love and joy into her life. An advocate for animal rights, Caroline urges all her readers to spay and neuter their pets. Unchecked reproduction causes pain and suffering for hundreds of thousands of innocent animals.

Books by Caroline Burnes

HARLEQUIN INTRIGUE

86—A DEADLY BREED
100—MEASURE OF DECEIT
115—PHANTOM FILLY
134—FEAR FAMILIAR*
154—THE JAGUAR'S EYE
186—DEADLY CURRENTS
204—FATAL INGREDIENTS
215—TOO FAMILIAR*
229—HOODWINKED
241—FLESH AND BLOOD
256—THRICE FAMILIAR*
267—CUTTING EDGE
277—SHADES OF FAMILIAR*
293—FAMILIAR REMEDY*
322—FAMILIAR TALE*
343—BEWITCHING FAMILIAR*
399—A CHRISTMAS KISS
409—MIDNIGHT PREY
426—FAMILIAR HEART*
452—FAMILIAR FIRE*
485—REMEMBER ME, COWBOY
502—FAMILIAR VALENTINE*

525—AFTER DARK
     "Familiar Stranger"*
542—FAMILIAR CHRISTMAS*
554—TEXAS MIDNIGHT
570—FAMILIAR OBSESSION*
614—FAMILIAR LULLABY*
635—MIDNIGHT BURNING
669—FAMILIAR MIRAGE†
673—FAMILIAR OASIS†
712—RIDER IN THE MIST**
715—BABE IN THE WOODS**
729—FAMILIAR DOUBLE*

*Fear Familiar
†Fear Familiar: Desert Mysteries
**The Legend of Blackthorn

Don't miss any of our special offers. Write to us at the following address for information on our newest releases.

Harlequin Reader Service
U.S.: 3010 Walden Ave., P.O. Box 1325, Buffalo, NY 14269
Canadian: P.O. Box 609, Fort Erie, Ont. L2A 5X3

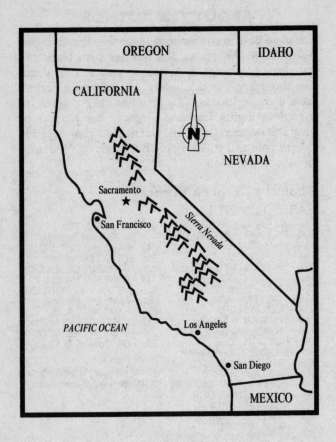

CAST OF CHARACTERS

Familiar—Putting aside his detective skills, Familiar signs on as a stunt double for a movie. On the set, though, he finds that mystery and intrigue aren't far way.

Nicole Paul—For twenty years Nicole has believed her father was convicted of a crime he didn't commit. When Nicole is also charged with stealing jewels, her job as a stuntwoman is threatened...and so is her heart.

Jax McClure—A stunt coordinator for the movie, Jax is drawn to the beautiful, reserved Nicole. And when she's set up for a fall, Jax steps in to protect her. Together they work to untangle a web of secrets that leads back to the theft of the cursed diamond, The Dream of Isis.

Vincent Paul—Twenty years ago, renowned jeweler Vincent was about to make his mark. Instead, he wound up in prison as a jewel thief. Now that he's out, it's his daughter who is in trouble.

Carlos Sanchez—A powerful lawyer, Carlos defended Nicole's father twenty years ago. Now, no matter where Nicole turns, Carlos pops up. Is it coincidence or something worse?

Monica Kane—Rich, beautiful and destined to be a success, Monica never achieved her goals of stardom. Once The Dream of Isis was stolen her career began to slide. Is it the curse at work?

John Hudson—A famed movie director, Hudson has a dark secret in his past. Does he possess a hidden motive for bringing Nicole and Monica together on the set of his new movie?

Allan Lancaster—He insured The Dream of Isis— and lost everything he valued when it was stolen. Is he out for revenge?

For Renee Paul, best friend and cat lover.
She has a tender heart for feline and human alike.

Chapter One

Being on a movie set is pretty cool. I mean there are babes everywhere. They bring in the food, they work on the cameras, they star in the film—and the biggest babe of them all isn't even the star. She's the stunt double. Miss Nicole Paul is one of the hottest bods I've seen in years—and she's just the stuntwoman and body double for Angela Myers.

I'm sure Peter and Eleanor, my humanoids, would send me back to the hotel room if they knew I was developing a fantasy about Nicole. But she's so dang gorgeous, with her long legs and silky blond hair. I mean she's fine. And nice, too, unlike Angela. They look enough alike to be sisters, but appearances are as far as it goes. Angela's a witch. She actually tried to swat me with a rolled-up script because I sniffed her grilled shrimp.

She was yelling at me, saying she was a b-i-g n-a-m-e and didn't have to put up with cat hair in her food. If Peter and Eleanor weren't consulting on the movie set about animal behavior, I would have been sent to the pound. As it is, I've got my own job *on the movie. I'm a body double for Elvis, the kitty star. He's a sleek black rascal with a far better attitude than his human costar. In fact, Elvis has a real sense of humor. I think we're going to become fast friends while I'm on this gig in Tinsel town.*

I hear the call for lights, camera, action. They're getting ready to film another scene for this movie about a cat who steals jewelry to bring people who love each other together. It's a charming plot. Reminds me of some things I've done in the past.

Wait, what is that? It's the police. And they're headed my way. No, they're passing me by and going to the trailer where Nicole is getting ready.

They're knocking on her door. She's opening it. And they're putting her in handcuffs. Let me just say that Nicole isn't acting docile about this. She's doing her best to get away from them, and she's one fit woman. I wouldn't want to take her on in a kickboxing match.

Everyone from the movie set is just standing around gawking. No one is doing a thing to help her. And we don't even know why she's being arrested.

This is an outrage. Why don't they cuff Angela? Speaking of which, she's standing in the doorway of her trailer and looking like the cat that swallowed the canary. Whatever is going on here, Angela definitely has a starring role in it.

I have two choices—to stay and perform my duties as a backup for Elvis, or to ride to the police station with Nicole. Since no one else is stepping up to help

her, I guess that leaves me. My decision is made. I'm
going to LAPD headquarters.

It's just a matter of timing to make it in the door
of the patrol car before they close it. Once I'm inside,
I don't think Nicole is going to give me away.

"YOU'RE ARRESTING the wrong person," Nicole said
through the screen of the patrol car. "I didn't steal
anything."

"We have a warrant for your arrest," the officer
who was driving said wearily. "Nothing personal,
lady, we're just doing our job."

"But I'm innocent," Nicole insisted. "Of course
that didn't matter twenty years ago, either."

The cop in the passenger seat turned around and
stared at her. "Twenty years ago, that would make
you, what, about twelve? What were you arrested for
then, robbing an ice-cream truck?"

Both police officers chuckled and Nicole threw
herself against the back seat of the car. This was
totally absurd. And the worst part of it was that she
hadn't seen it coming. Last night when Angela Myers had staged such a drama about the theft of her
precious earring, Nicole should have known that the
finger of blame would swing in her direction. Angela
had all but come out and said that Nicole was a thief,
just like her father. She'd implied that thievery was
a genetic trait. But Nicole had just shrugged it off.
She didn't think that anyone would believe she'd
steal anything. Now she saw differently. That's exactly what everyone thought, even the police.

She felt something against her leg and almost screamed. Before she could utter a sound, though, the sleek black cat put a paw on her knee and drilled her with a steady green gaze.

"Familiar?" she whispered. She knew it wasn't Elvis. As much as she enjoyed the black cat starring in the movie, he didn't have half the personality of the stunt cat that had been brought in with the movie consultants. Familiar was the easiest animal she'd ever worked with in setting up stunts.

"Meow," he said softly.

"So you came with me." She held her elbow steady as the cat rubbed against it. "I don't know why you did, but I'm glad you're here." She lifted her cuffed hands and let him jump into her lap. "We have to figure out a way to make them believe I didn't steal anything."

She stared into the cat's unblinking gaze and had the oddest sensation that he understood every word she said.

JAX MCCLURE WATCHED as the police officers came out of Nicole's trailer. They went straight over to Angela's, knocked, and when she opened the door, they held up a clear plastic bag with a glittering piece of jewelry.

"That's mine," Angela said. "I told you she stole it. She's been staring at those earrings every time I put them on. I told Mr. Hudson not to hire her on this set, but he wouldn't listen to me. Now, I guess he'll have to find someone to replace her in the middle of the film.''

Jax ignored most of Angela's rant. After five weeks of filming with her, he was more than ready to blow her up in some of the special effects he designed for the movie. She was one of the most difficult women he'd ever worked with—totally immune to his charm and totally wrapped up in herself. And Angela had had it in for Nicole ever since the stunt double walked onto the set of *Midnight Magic*.

Angela didn't even like the cat costar, Elvis. And Elvis was an easy cat to like.

Jax waited until the dust cleared and Angela was back in her trailer before he walked over to the police detectives.

"I'm a friend of Ms. Paul's," he said, which was stretching the truth quite a bit. Nicole had not been unfriendly, but she'd simply been unavailable for any of the crew get-togethers that might have forged the bond of friendship. She was a real loner. "Is she going to be charged?"

"Theft of property," the policeman said. "Ms. Myers didn't want to press burglary charges. She just wants her property back."

"Was there any sign of forced entry at Ms. Myer's trailer?" Jax asked.

The policeman shook his head. "We didn't look. No point if she won't press charges. The theft charge will be enough to send her away for a while."

Jax nodded. "Where is Ms. Paul being held?"

"County jail. She'll be arraigned as soon as possible

and then remanded somewhere else, unless she makes bail.''

"Thanks," Jax said. He walked back to the trailer he shared with another stuntman, Jason Thompson. There was something about the situation that didn't sit well with him. Nicole wasn't overly friendly, but he'd never seen her looking at the jewelry some of the stars wore. In fact, Nicole seemed to care very little about the things that normally turned a woman's head—jewelry, clothes, fancy cars, money. Now that he thought about it, she hadn't shown interest in any of those things.

Something about the theft just didn't jell.

He entered his trailer and took a bottle of cold water from the small refrigerator.

"Jason?" he called out.

"What?" His roommate came out of the back, his lean frame in cowboy boots, jeans and a button-down shirt. He was headed out on the town.

"What's the story on Nicole Paul?" Jax asked.

"Not much story on her. She's worked a few movie sets and done a fine job. She's just breaking into the business. The story is her old man."

"Her husband?"

"No, her father. He went up for some big jewelry heist back in the eighties. Seems like he was designing jewelry for all of the movie stars for the Academy Awards and some very important diamond disappeared." Jason scratched his chin. "Yeah, it was some lavender diamond. They called it the Dream of Isis. It was supposed to be cursed or some such. Anyway, Nicole's dad did some hard time over that jewel. I don't think he's been out of prison all that long. I hear he's in poor health. Bad ticker.''

"Was the diamond ever found?" Jax asked.

"Nope. Not a hint of it. And Nicole's old man— I think his name was Vincent—anyway, he never spoke of it again. At least that's the gossip that blows over the set and you'd know it if you ever talked to any of the extras. It's too bad for Nicole, though. Wherever she goes, someone resurrects that story about her dad.''

"What do you make of what happened today?

Jason shrugged. "Looks like the kid has a lot of her old man in her. Maybe she just got tired of being accused of things.''

"Or maybe someone went to a lot of trouble to make it look that way and set her up." Jax drank the rest of his water as he watched his roommate step out into the gathering dusk.

NICOLE USED HER one phone call to let her father know she was okay.

"I'll get you out as soon as possible," Vincent promised her. "I'm sorry, Nicole. This is more about me than you.''

"What do you mean?" Nicole felt a sudden rush of dread. Her father had just been released from prison. His health was not good. Was something else going on?

"I mean that you've been tarred with the brush of

thief because of me,'' he said slowly. ''You're accused because of me.''

''That's not true! This isn't about anyone except
Angela Myers. She planted that earring in my trailer.
I just don't know why. What does she gain by getting
me off the set? They'll have to slow filming until
they find a new double.''

There was a long silence on the other end. ''We
need to talk as soon as you get out,'' Vincent said.
''I'll see if I can get Carlos on the phone. You're
going to need a lawyer and he's one of the best.''

''We can't afford Carlos,'' Nicole said tersely. The
last thing she needed to do was put her father under
financial pressure. ''This is a mistake. They'll
straighten it out.''

She heard the silence on her father's end. She was
echoing the words he'd said twenty years before
when he'd been charged—and wrongly convicted—
of the theft of the Dream of Isis. Back then, they'd
both been certain that the authorities would rectify
their tragic mistake. But they hadn't, and Vincent had
gone to prison for a long, long time.

''We can't count on that,'' Vincent said in a voice
low and worried. ''Talk to Carlos. He'll help you say
the right things. And don't talk to the police. That
was one of the biggest mistakes I made. Every single
thing I said was twisted and turned against me.''

''I remember,'' Nicole said. She'd been twelve,
and it had been impossible to forget. Her beloved
father, her only parent after her mother's death when
she was nine, had been painted as a thief all over

town. The only thing that had saved her was that she'd gone to live with an aunt in Nebraska. She'd been able to leave the crime behind, sort of. Her father had never had that luxury.

"Promise me, Nicole," Vincent said.

"I promise." She hung up the phone and let the guard take her back to the cell she shared with three other women.

As soon as the door shut, one of the women nodded toward the top bunk. "My name is Connie, and you've got a visitor."

Nicole looked up to see the green eyes of the cat staring at her. "What are you doing here?" she asked the cat.

"We don't know," Connie said. "He slipped in here, checked things out and then hopped into that bunk. He's been watching, like he was expecting you. What kind of cat is he?"

Nicole couldn't help but smile. She was in jail and what she'd done wrong wasn't the question anyone was interested in.

"If I remember correctly, he was a stray that a veterinarian and his wife saved from animal experimentation. Then it turned out he's smarter than your average person. He's solved mysteries all over the world, and right now he's working as a stunt double for a cat on a movie set."

"You've got to be kidding me," Connie said, reaching up to stroke the cat. "What's he doing here?"

"He works with me," Nicole said, and for some

reason she couldn't explain, just having Familiar around made her feel a whole lot better.

"The guards won't let you keep him," Connie said. She leaned closer to Nicole. "Neither will Lizzie." She nodded in the direction of a tall, muscular girl. "She doesn't like cats or dogs or people."

"I won't be here that long," Nicole said. "I'm innocent."

The laughter from Lizzie and the as-yet-unidentified woman was loud and raucous. "Yeah, we're all innocent, sweetheart."

Nicole didn't argue. She knew better. She'd been stupid to shoot her mouth off, as if these women really cared whether she was a thief or not.

"What are you charged with?" she asked Connie.

"Grand theft auto." She looked down at the floor. "The car was mine. My boyfriend gave it to me for my birthday."

"She didn't get the paperwork, just the key. The car was never registered in her name," Lizzie said, laughing. "Sucker."

"I'm sure you'll be able to explain it." Nicole had enough on her plate.

"Kevin says he's going to let me rot in here because I wanted to break up with him. He has the car and I'm stuck here. He says he has the best of both worlds."

Nicole didn't know what to say. "Did you get a lawyer?"

"Public defender, but he seems okay." She finally

looked up, pushing her hair out of her eyes. "Awful young to be a lawyer."

"How old are you?" Nicole found herself asking, though she didn't really want to know. She didn't want to be involved at even the most basic level.

"Eighteen."

"What about your parents?" she asked.

"What about them?" Connie's bravado faded as quickly as it had come. "They're in Arkansas. I haven't talked to them since I left three years ago."

"And you came out to L.A. to be an actress, right?" Nicole asked, feeling as if she'd dropped into the middle of a really awful B movie. *Women in Prison* or something like that.

"I know it sounds stupid, but I really can act."

"And pigs can fly," Lizzie said, creating another round of laughter.

The guard came for Nicole. "You've been bonded out," he said.

"Just a minute," Nicole said. She gave one desperate look around the cell, then leaned over to Connie and whispered something.

WHO WOULD HAVE THOUGHT I'd end up in a cell with four prisoners. But it could be worse. Nicole is drop-dead gorgeous and I get the feeling that Connie wouldn't look half-bad if she had a little meat on her bones and some decent clothes. Now, that Lizzie is another matter. She'd scare the paint off a fence.

Nicole is getting out of here and I'm curious to see who made her bond. There's another little matter to consider. I'm AWOL from the movie set and by now my humanoids have missed me. Maybe I should get on the phone to Eleanor and Peter and let them know where I am.

While I'm here, it might be a good idea for me to take a look at the report filed by the detective investigating the case. And I wonder who that might be? I guess I came off a little half-cocked, but I wanted Nicole to know she wasn't alone. I don't know why, but I thought that was important.

Here we go. She's scooping me into her arms. Looks like we're out of here. But she's giving Connie a phone number to call. She's going to help Connie, too. Now, that's the ticket.

I hear the chow cart. I'd say let's stay for a meal, but somehow I know better than to get my hopes up. I am a cat with discriminating taste, and prison food just doesn't have the appeal that a steak does.

I have to say the checkout process is fast here. But look who's come to take Nicole home. It sure isn't her daddy. My, oh, my, I think there's going to be some serious trouble.

Chapter Two

Jax saw Nicole balk as soon as she saw him. He hooked his boot heel on the chair rail and cocked a hip, playing it cool. What in the hell was he doing here? He'd acted on impulse, thinking that he'd sashay up to the jailhouse and get Nicole out, and that she'd be grateful to him. Judging by the look on her face, she was anything but grateful. He made sure his body was relaxed, striking a pose as she started toward him again. He raised his eyebrows when he saw the black cat at her heels.

"What's the cat charged with? Is he a cat burglar?" he asked the desk clerk, earning several laughs from officers in the area.

"Maybe we should book him for consorting with a prisoner," the sergeant said. "I don't know how he got in here, but it's a good thing he's headed out. We don't have animals in the jail. At least not the four-legged kind."

"Well, he has good taste," Jax commented. He turned to Nicole. "I came to give you a ride back to the set. We've got the action shot scheduled tonight and we can't do it without you.''

He saw a series of emotions shift across her expressive face. One was relief, the other disappointment.

''Did John Hudson put up my bail money?''

Jax hesitated. He was tempted to answer in the affirmative, even though it wasn't true. ''John doesn't know you were arrested. He wasn't on the set today.''

''You came on your own?'' Her surprise was evident in her voice.

''I did. We need you on the set. As stunt coordinator, my butt's on the line if we get behind schedule.''

Nicole didn't say anything. She took her personal belongings from the envelope the desk sergeant handed her. ''We'd better get this scene shot, then. Once John Hudson knows I've been arrested for stealing jewelry from the cast, he's going to fire me.''

Jax couldn't deny that. Hudson probably would fire her—if that was all there was to the story. But Jax had a hunch there was something else going on. ''John Hudson's a fair man. If there's another side to the story, he'll listen.''

''I was framed,'' Nicole said simply.

''Who would frame you and why?'' Jax asked. It was a logical question, but he saw instantly that it annoyed her.

''If I knew the answer to that, I'd know how to

start clearing my name,'' Nicole said, heading out the door.

"Do you have any idea?'' Jax asked. Even though he took long strides, he had to hustle to catch up with her. Nicole was long limbed and moving fast. But he couldn't help but appreciate the rear view as she stalked away.

"Well, logically, I'd start with Angela Myers. It was her earring that was stolen and found in my trailer. I know I didn't take it, but someone did. And that someone put it right where the cops could find it. And I'd be willing to lay you some pretty good odds that Angela told the police to search my trailer. I just wonder how she knew the earring was there if she didn't put it there herself.''

"Why would Angela want to frame you as a thief?'' Jax asked. He knew the women didn't care for each other. The truth was, Angela didn't care for anyone except herself—and whoever was the focus of her narcissistic passion.

"Because she's psychotic?'' Nicole asked with a heaping measure of sarcasm. "Because she's mean? Or maybe because she doesn't want to finish this film? I hear she got an offer from Paramount for a starring role in a drama that she's itching to do. There's a little time problem. She can't finish this film and be on that set, too. If this movie were to shut down, she'd be free to rush right over to Paramount and become the belle of the studio.''

Jax pushed open the outer door for Nicole. "You

really think Angela would wreck the entire movie just to get out of her contract?''

Nicole stopped dead and turned. She didn't say a word; she only raised her eyebrows.

''Well, she is pretty self-centered,'' Jax admitted. He saw the first hint of a smile at the corners of Nicole's mouth. Before he could be certain of it, though, she bent down and swept the black cat into her arms.

''This cat's a detective,'' she said. ''I read all about him. He's going to help me figure out what's going on here.''

''I'll help, too.'' Jax almost wanted to duck when he spoke the words. Nicole's face showed extreme surprise, and then wariness.

''Why would you help me?'' she asked.

''I don't know. Maybe because I'm a sucker for the underdog. It's a fine Texas tradition. Started at the Alamo, you know. All Texans like long odds. Or maybe it's because I don't think you stole the earring.''

''And why do you think I'm innocent?''

That question alone told him volumes about the kind of life Nicole had led. Her father's conviction and incarceration had become part of her personality. Whether folks in the past had judged Nicole guilty by association, or whether it was just her interpretation of events, he couldn't tell. But he did know she didn't expect support from anyone. She'd learned to live life by her own wits.

He took a deep breath. "You're building a solid career as a stuntwoman. You're good at your job. You do your work and you do it with pride. I just don't see you ruining all of this over some bauble."

Nicole's jaw muscle worked as she listened to him. "I didn't steal anything. I'm not a thief."

"I believe you," he said. "That's why I'm offering to help you."

"Meow!" The black cat put a paw on Nicole's shoulder as if to say "Me, too."

"I don't know exactly what we're going to do, though," Nicole said and her shoulders slumped a little. "The police found the earring in my trailer. They'll never believe someone else put it there."

"I have a couple of ideas," Jax said, pointing to a pickup truck that was parked up the street. "But first we're going back to the set and you're going to finish that stunt."

"I can't do that," Nicole said, putting on the brakes. Jax felt the resistance of a boulder as he gently took her elbow to move her forward.

"You have to," he said, inching her toward the truck.

"They all think I'm a thief," she said. "I can't go back there."

"So prove them wrong. Don't act guilty. We'll finish the scene and then maybe we'll have some time left over to ask a few questions. Maybe someone saw something."

Nicole gave in and got in the passenger side of the truck, placing Familiar on her lap.

Jax was grinning as he walked around the truck. By the time he got in it, he'd managed to control his expression. He knew Nicole wouldn't take lightly to the idea that he was amused by her. But for the past three weeks, since the movie had started shooting, he'd thought she was such a tough loner. Now he found out different. Her tough act was just a way to disguise her insecurities.

Oh, well, Hollywood was the town of facade. But no matter what image Nicole projected, he didn't see her as a thief. About the only thing he'd suspect her of stealing was someone's heart. Lucky for him he was immune in that department. He'd paid out his heart a long time ago when he'd gambled and lost. Still, it was the Texas thing to do—rescue a damsel in distress. Hell, it was just the way he was brought up.

When he felt the grin creeping back onto his face, he wiped it off. Nicole was watching him with open curiosity, as was the black cat. He'd never heard that Familiar was a detective, but after watching the feline on the set, he'd believe Familiar was capable of anything. Anything at all.

NICOLE BALANCED OUTSIDE the window of the three-story house, Familiar at her side. She didn't look down. It was a long drop, and even though the air-filled bags were there to catch her if she fell, she didn't like the sickening sensation of dropping that distance. Familiar, with his claws in the siding of the house, had no intention of falling.

"Just a few more steps," she whispered encouragement to the cat.

The spotlight on the ground swept over her and she froze, hoping that she looked like a black shadow amongst the other shadows of the house. That was what the script called for, and she could only hope that the lighting was correct. She didn't want to hang around thirty feet above the ground while John and the crew worked through technical difficulties.

The spotlight moved on, and she let out a breath. Apparently all the technical aspects were working fine. The first shots, where she'd scaled the exterior wall of the house, had gone off without a hitch. Now she was waiting for the director to signal her into the window. Of course, the exterior had been spiked with handholds and footholds for her safety. Familiar had been added to the scene later.

"Move to the window," John Hudson called out to her.

Following his direction, she eased to the window and slowly raised it. Per the script, a gossamer curtain drifted out and surrounded her. In another moment she felt Jax's strong arms lift her into the building and to safety. He also gave Familiar an assist into the house.

"That was terrific," Jax told her. "John was able to get it clean with only one shot."

"Thank goodness. I don't want to have to do that again."

"You're not afraid of heights, are you?" Jax teased.

"I'm not afraid of them, but I'm not in love with them either." Nicole found that she was smiling at him. The entire time she'd been getting ready for her action scene she'd been thinking of him. She could still recall his oh-so-relaxed pose in the jail. But he'd shown up to help her and he didn't even know her.

"Jax, thanks for this afternoon. I'll pay you back the bond money. It'll take me a little while, but I'll pay back every penny of it."

Jax didn't say anything. He just looked at her. "I'm not in a bind for cash right now. Don't worry about it."

"But I will return the money. I always pay my debts."

"I'm sure you will." He gathered up some rope and gear and walked to the window, signaling down to the director. "Okay?"

"Perfect!" John called up to him. "Absolutely perfect. Tell Nicole she gets the gold star for the day."

"You can tell her yourself," Jax said. He turned to Nicole. "This is a perfect opportunity for you to explain what happened today. John will listen and be fair."

He was handing her a chance to save her job. Maybe. Or it could just be an opportunity to get thrown off the set in front of the entire film crew. At least Angela wasn't around.

"Do you want me to talk to him?" Jax asked.

Once again she was amazed at his willingness to put himself on the line for her. "No," she said carefully. "This is my problem. You've already gone out on a limb getting me out of jail. What if something else goes missing?"

"That's a risk I'm willing to take."

She felt a rush of tears and blinked them back. She hadn't cried since she was twelve years old and had watched her father being escorted into jail. "I'll talk to John. And I'll do it right now."

She lifted her shoulders and held her head high as she walked out of the set house and over to a battery of cameras. John Hudson sat among the expensive machinery, his speculative gaze focused on the house.

"Films today are all about action, Nicole. You know that, I know that, but why is it that I just long to tell a good story?" His grin was ironic as he patted the chair next to him. "The camera loves you, Nicole. Let an old man give you some advice. Start reading for the female leads. You're good enough to get them. And a lot less trouble than our current female star."

"John, I was arrested today for stealing Angela's earring. The cops found it in my dressing trailer."

John Hudson's craggy and wrinkled face was part of Hollywood lore. He slowly turned to Nicole and looked at her. "I remember when your father was arrested for stealing the Dream of Isis. I never believed he did it. But he was convicted and sent to prison."

He let his words hang between them.

"I didn't take the earring. I had no reason to take it."

"How did it get in your trailer?"

She shook her head. "I don't know."

"What do you suspect?"

She started to tell him that Angela was quite capable of framing her and why—her new movie offer. But she held her tongue. She had no evidence against Angela, and she knew what it felt like to be falsely accused.

"I really don't know. All I do know is that I'm innocent. I didn't take it."

John nodded. "I have your word on it."

"You do." She almost added "For what it's worth," but she didn't. John was doing his best to be square with her. He didn't deserve her caustic remarks.

"Have you hired a lawyer?"

She shook her head. "My father recommended Carlos Sanchez."

"He defended your father." John nodded slowly. "Okay, then let's get back to work. I want to finish this sequence, then you have a costume change. We'll do the scene on the balcony with the evening gown."

"Tonight?" Nicole wasn't prepared for that scene. It wasn't scheduled to be shot for at least another week, and it was one of the trickiest shots of the movie, at least for her.

"Yes, right away. I'll tell everyone to begin to prepare. I want this scene in the can."

He walked away to consult with a cameraman and

Nicole was left sitting alone. She finished John's thought. He wanted this scene in the can before she was carted off to jail.

JAX SIPPED the cold beer. Normally he wasn't a beer-drinking man, but it was hard to fit in with the cast and crew without occasionally drinking a brew. Especially when a card game was as hot and heavy as this one.

He threw in another fifty-dollar chip and called the bet. His cards, tightly folded together, were held loosely in his hand. Unless the gods of luck were truly against him, he had the winning hand that would bring home a five-hundred-dollar pot. He'd always been lucky at cards, horses and escaping injury. Now, women were another story.

Two men dropped out, leaving Jax, the male lead Kyle Lancer, and O. J. Adams, the cinematographer.

"Well, well, looks like lucky Jax has done it to you boys again."

They all looked up to see Angela standing at the door. She was wearing a red evening gown. "I thought I might find you boys here. I guess you forgot you were supposed to show up for the publicity shots, Kyle."

"I didn't forget. I decided not to do it. Besides, I wouldn't want to come between you and your love affair with the camera."

A couple of the guys started to laugh but stopped when Angela walked into the room. She moved like a panther. She was just as beautiful and just as deadly.

"You left me waiting there for you like a fool. I don't appreciate it."

"Sorry, Angela. I thought I was doing you a favor."

"That's the problem with you, Kyle. You aren't equipped to think. That requires a working brain. You're just one handsome hunk of muscle. So in the future, don't think. Just show up and do what you're told." She whipped around and left the room, leaving a faint trail of perfume that smelled like gardenias.

O.J. took in a deep breath. "Wow, she smells like flowers, but sulfur would be more appropriate."

The men laughed. Jax still held his cards, biding his time.

"Well, it's show time, boys," Kyle said, putting two pair on the table. "Who can beat it?"

O.J. threw his cards facedown. "Not me."

Just as Kyle was reaching for the pot, Jax laid his cards down faceup. The three queens were offset by a pair of threes.

"Full house," Jax said, pulling the money toward his place. "I was running a little low on cash. Thanks, boys."

"Yeah, we heard you made bond on Nicole."

Even though Jax was startled by O.J.'s comment, he didn't show it. In many respects, Hollywood was a small town. Folks in the business heard lots of rumors, but most of them were untrue. This time someone had actually gotten the facts straight.

"I needed her to work this evening."

"She's good at her job," O.J. said, grinning. "Is she good at anything else?"

"Now, that's something I can't answer." Jax felt

instant annoyance at the insinuation in O.J.'s comment. But he knew the cinematographer well enough to know he was only cutting up, as all the men did when they weren't around the women. Still, he was amazed to find he was a little prickly where Nicole's honor was at stake. "Where'd you hear it?"

O.J. looked at the pile of money in front of Jax. "I'll play you for the details. That pot against what I know." He grinned wickedly.

"I don't want to know that bad. I'll just wait for breakfast and it'll be all over the set."

"Rumors do fly," another of the men commented.

"I'm out of here." Kyle stood up, stretching. "Same time tomorrow night?"

"Don't count on me," Jax said, standing also.

"Hey, you can't wipe us out and not give us a chance to win it back," O.J. complained.

"I'll be back," Jax said, grinning. "Eventually."

"Where's the fire?" O.J. asked, eyebrows lifted. "Or should I say, where's the hot stuff?"

"I only wish my life was as exciting as you seem to believe it is," Jax said in his easy drawl. "I've got to set up a harness for that shot in the ravine." He didn't wait for them to tease him more, he simply left. Part of what he said was true, but there were other things on his agenda, too. Like keeping tabs on a tall, leggy blonde.

Chapter Three

Jax leaned against the side of Kyle Lancer's trailer and waited. He'd been there twenty minutes and Angela was still inside. He could only wonder what she was up to. Sleeping with Kyle was a possibility, but it certainly didn't seem to be her style.

Kyle was rich and handsome, but he was dumb as a post. Hollywood lore portrayed Angela as something of a black widow. She liked her men smarter—more fun to toy with before she ate them. Then again, he'd only heard rumors. He really knew nothing at all about Angela except that she was a total witch. She seemed to take pleasure in belittling people, and for the past five weeks, Nicole had been on the receiving end of her abuse. It had become a real point of curiosity to him why Angela hated Nicole so much. He suspected jealousy, but he had nothing to base that on except that he felt Nicole was a far better actress than Angela. And Nicole didn't even consider herself to be an actress. She viewed herself only as a stuntwoman. Well, Nicole could give Angela a serious run for her money in a contest for movie roles.

The door cracked and he heard Angela's voice.

"Don't ever stand me up like that again, Kyle."

If she'd gone to see Kyle for some romance, it had ended on a sour note. Jax pressed himself deeper into the shadows. The last thing he wanted was for Angela to see him. He wasn't concerned about catching the rough side of her tongue, but he didn't want her to know he was following her.

"Or what?" Kyle asked, his voice slightly slurred.

"Or you'll pay a heavy price."

Kyle laughed. "What are you gonna do, get me fired?" He laughed louder. "I'm carrying this movie. John won't fire me, but he could damn sure send you down the road if I made a big enough stink about it. In fact, that pretty stuntwoman—"

"You shut your mouth," Angela snapped. "You're a fool, Kyle. Nicole Paul's only talent is with sticky fingers. She's an exceptional thief, just like her father. I don't think that's what John Hudson is looking for. And I wouldn't count on John as an ally on this. We have a special relationship."

"John Hudson's far too smart to sleep with you, Angela. And from what I've seen on the set, that may be the only acting talent you have."

"You're disgusting," Angela said with more scorn than she'd ever put into delivering lines.

"Just because you think you've landed a big fish from the studio doesn't mean your career is going to take off. Take my advice, Angela. Gig that fish, get him in the boat and get a ring on your finger."

"I don't need a ring. I'm going to be a star."

Kyle laughed. "You're just another pretty face, darling. A pretty face and a bad disposition. Your days are numbered."

"You're a pathetic drunk."

"I must have been drunk to sign on to this picture with you. I guess I thought you might still have a soft spot for me." His laughter was ugly. "What do you think your powerful lover would think if he knew the truth about you?"

"You don't have the guts to tell him."

"Oh, don't I?"

"No, you don't. If you open your mouth, you'll never work in this town again and you know it."

"You're just full of empty threats, Angela. Maybe I've had enough. Maybe I'm ready to call your bluff."

"You're going to be sorry!" Angela stormed out of the trailer, slamming the door shut so hard it bounced open again. In a moment she was down the stairs and striding across the parking lot in her spiked heels.

To Jax's intense amusement, her heel collapsed and she almost fell down.

"Damn him to hell," she raged. She slipped off the shoe and hobbled back to her trailer.

Jax followed at a discreet distance. He checked his watch. With a twisted ankle, he didn't think Angela would be running out any more that night. He could finally go home and go to bed.

He lingered outside for another fifteen minutes, just to make sure that no one went to see Angela.

He couldn't have said why he'd chosen to shadow the star instead of Nicole. But after the arduous stunts he and Nicole had completed for shooting that night, he had no doubt that Nicole was in her trailer sound asleep. As he should be.

Sauntering across the parking lot, he took note that everyone had settled in for the night. A movie set was a lot like a neighborhood. There were good neighbors and bad. Some of the younger cast members had a tendency to stay up too late and be too noisy, but it was all part of moviemaking.

On his way to his trailer, he passed Nicole's. He was surprised to see a light burning. When he'd gone by earlier, it had been dark. An unpleasant sensation curled through him. Had he been following the wrong blonde? No, he couldn't believe that. And Nicole wasn't stupid enough to advertise her movements by turning lights on and off. No, if she was up to anything, she'd be more discreet about it.

He was about to walk on when he saw her silhouette pass by the window. Her long hair was tumbled down her back and she stopped for a moment and drank a glass of something. Even in shadow form she was a beautiful woman. Beautiful and challenging. Just the way he liked them. She turned abruptly away and he was left with only an empty window.

NICOLE PUT DOWN the water glass she'd been drinking from and picked up the telephone receiver that had suddenly started to ring. No one ever called her. And certainly no one called her so late at night.

She answered and then felt her heart jolt. It was her father. She held the phone in her hand so tightly that her knuckles were white.

"Daddy, are you okay?"

"I'm not feeling well, Nicole. I hate to call you in the middle of the night, but I'm afraid I need you."

"I'm on my way," Nicole said, pulling on jeans and shoes as she talked.

"Drive safely," Vincent Paul said in a weak voice. "I couldn't take it if something happened to you."

"I'm fine, Dad. I'll be careful. Just try to relax. Shall I call an ambulance?"

"No, no ambulance. Not yet."

"Can you tell me what happened?"

"I think I just got upset and my blood pressure got too high. I'm okay, Nicole, but it would be good to see you."

She snatched up a blouse and searched through a pile of things for a bra. She was a terrible housekeeper. She could never seem to find time to put things where they belonged. It was a habit that would drive her father nuts. He was such a neat-nick.

"Dad, can you call your doctor?"

"I don't think it's necessary, Nicole. In fact, just talking to you has made me feel better. It really isn't necessary that you come over here."

"Too late to avoid me now," she said, putting a light note on it. "I'm on my way. Besides, I want to talk to you about what happened today. I don't want you to worry about it.'' This was, she felt certain, at the root of her father's heart flare-up. He'd been worried about her and it had affected his health.

"Okay, but just drive carefully."

"I'm headed out the door, Daddy. I'll be there in half an hour."

JAX HAD WATCHED the production of her dressing, and he'd felt only a brief moment of guilt. He hadn't meant to be a voyeur, but once he started watching, he couldn't force himself to leave. He was still standing in the shadows when the trailer door opened and Nicole came flying out and jumped into her car.

She'd barely gotten the door closed before she was turning the key. The engine turned over but didn't catch. She tried to start it again with the same result.

Jax hesitated. Wherever Nicole was going, she seemed in a major hurry. And she seemed upset. But he wasn't certain she would appreciate his help. Then again, he'd never know unless he asked her.

He let her try the car several times before he walked over to the old coupe and tapped on the window.

Again he saw a wash of emotions on her face as she recognized him. At first there was what appeared to be happy surprise, then amazement and finally wariness.

"Sounds like your electrical system is out of whack. Maybe something as simple as a spark plug. Want me to check it?"

He saw the internal struggle. Nicole had a really hard time accepting help from anyone.

"My father's ill," she finally said. "I have to get there fast."

He opened the door. "Forget this. I'll drive you, or you can take my motorcycle. Come on."

Nicole didn't argue. She got out of the car and followed him.

"You could use the truck, but Jason borrowed it and I know he isn't back yet. He never gets in until the wee hours." He led the way through a maze of trailers until he stopped at a huge black motorcycle. From his jeans he pulled out the key and extended it to Nicole. "Helmet's on the back."

She shook her head. "I've never driven one of these."

Jax nodded. He handed her the helmet that hung from the backrest and reached for another in a storage box beside the bike. "Come on, then. I'll drive you wherever you need to go."

He had already swung his leg over the bike and straddled it when he felt her hand on his arm. "Why are you doing this?" she asked.

"Doing what?"

"Being nice to me. Helping me. Why?"

Jax found that he really didn't have an answer to her question. He hadn't analyzed his reasons. At least not in any sensible way. All he knew was that Nicole had gotten more than one rough break in life. Maybe it *was* just a Texas thing to stand up for the underdog. It could even be that he enjoyed the courage and spirit she showed on the job. She tackled things that frightened her, and she did it without complaint. Or maybe it was simply because she was one of the most beautiful women he'd ever seen. Angela Myers and Nicole could have passed for sisters.

Angela was a beautiful woman, but she lacked something that Nicole possessed. He couldn't pin it down—yet—but he knew one thing for certain. He wanted a chance to spend time with Nicole so that he could figure it out.

He felt Nicole swing a leg over the seat and press against him. He turned the ignition switch and felt the engine purr to life. As he pushed off, he felt Nicole's arms go around his chest. Involuntarily she clung to him as the powerful bike surged forward.

Jax grinned to himself. Sometimes real life was even better than fantasy.

NICOLE CLOSED her eyes and pressed hard against Jax as he took one of the hairpin curves at sixty miles an hour. The bike leaned down, hugging the curve, and she did her best to shift her body weight with Jax.

Beneath the fear of the ride was a deep excitement. She'd never ridden a motorcycle like this one. In a few movie scenes she'd had to ride a smaller dirt bike for several hundred yards and then lay it down in a patch of sand. That experience hadn't been nearly this exhilarating.

And part of the excitement was Jax. Where had he

suddenly come from? And why was he being so kind to her? In her life there had been one or two men who'd made overtures of friendship and kindness, but in the end there was always a price tag attached. A big one. Nicole had made a vow a long time ago that she wasn't about to pay that price for anyone's help. She could do perfectly well on her own.

Jax took a left turn down a darkened canyon road, and Nicole had to admit that he knew his way around town. Vincent Paul lived in a small house tucked away on one of the cliffs overhanging the Malibu colony. When he'd first moved there, decades before, the property had been cheap. Now it was the only thing he owned that was worth anything. Several times Nicole had urged him to sell it and move closer into Los Angeles proper.

His reply had been that his canyon home was the one thing that kept him going in prison. All he could think about was getting out and returning to the place where he'd been happily married and the father of a young girl. Now he was determined to live out the rest of his life in that place.

Nicole had given up fighting the strength of his memories, but as she sped through the night on the back of Jax's motorcycle, she wished she'd been more insistent. If Vincent was having a heart attack, the ambulance would never get there in time.

She leaned into another curve with Jax and felt the bike slow as they approached the narrow gravel driveway that wound up to the house.

Jax eased the bike up the gravel as Nicole held her breath and prayed they didn't slide backward. But in a few seconds they were pulling up beside the house and parking.

As she got off, her legs visibly trembled. She felt Jax's hand on her arm as he steadied her. "You're a helluva passenger," he said as he removed his helmet. "You balanced perfectly on the curves. You're a natural on a bike."

"Thanks," she said. She watched as he rubbed one hand over his unruly blond hair. She handed him the helmet. "Let me see how bad my father is."

She didn't wait for an answer. She hurried into the house, using her key. "Daddy?" she called, walking through the kitchen and then the den. "Daddy?" It was a small two-bedroom house. Her former room had been on this floor and her parents had shared the bedroom beneath. It had been built so that it hung off the face of the cliff.

"Daddy?" She ran through the house, taking the stairs so fast she almost tripped.

"I'm in here."

She hurried into the bedroom to find her father stretched out on the bed. He wore jeans and a turtleneck and looked every inch the European artist that he was, even though his face was pale.

"What's wrong?" she asked, rushing forward to put a hand on his forehead and then to grab his wrist to check his pulse.

"I just had a little scare," he said.

"What kind of scare?"

"I was afraid I was having a heart attack, but I feel a little better now. I'm sorry that I frightened you, Nicole. You must have flown here."

"Almost," she admitted with a slow grin. Her father's pulse was elevated, but with each passing second she could see that he was recovering. "What got you upset, Dad?"

Vincent shook his head. "I can't really say. You know how these medical things are. No rhyme or reason to them."

Nicole noticed that her father wasn't looking at her when he talked. Even after twenty years in prison, Vincent shared an extraordinary ability to communicate with his daughter. They'd always been able to simply sit across from each other and tell the truth about whatever was happening in their lives. She remembered clearly when Vincent had called her into the kitchen to tell her that he'd been accused of stealing the Dream of Isis. He'd told her flat out, and then he'd also told her that he didn't do it, but that he was going to be tried as a thief. He'd never sugarcoated a single bit of it, and she'd never doubted that he was innocent.

"Dad, you aren't telling me the truth," she said softly. "What really happened?"

Vincent looked up at her. "Nicole, I spoke to Carlos Sanchez for you. He's willing to take the case."

"Daddy! We can't afford Carlos. He's one of the biggest names in Los Angeles. I'll get a public defender. I'm not guilty and we don't have the money to spend on someone like Carlos." She didn't bother to point out that paying Carlos Sanchez for defending her father had wiped out every bit of their savings. They'd sold cars, jewelry, tools, furnishings—everything except the house.

And Carlos had lost the case.

"I've already talked to him. He's going to handle everything. He's always felt guilty about not winning my case, though we all know that I convicted myself by talking to the police so freely," Vincent said. "You need a big name, Nicole. Carlos Sanchez has become a man of great power. I want you to let him help you." He sat up on the bed. "Why don't we have a glass of wine and you can tell me everything that happened?"

"Dad, someone brought me here. My car wouldn't start. He's waiting out in the yard. Let me go and tell him that it's okay to leave me here."

"Who is this?" Vincent asked. "A boyfriend?"

Nicole shook her head, knowing that her father wanted nothing more than for her to find true love and happiness. "No, he isn't a boyfriend. He's a…co-worker. Actually, when you get right down to it, he's my boss."

She followed behind her father. As he slowly climbed the stairs, she was reminded again that she should continue to press Vincent to sell the house. He'd be safer in a one-level closer to the medical center.

Before she could stop him, Vincent went to the door and called out into the night. "Young man! Come inside for a glass of wine. My daughter, as usual, has made my ailments more serious than they are.''

"Father!" Nicole was outraged. "You called me and scared me half to death and now I'm the one who's exaggerating things?"

Vincent grinned at her, signaling Jax into the house. "Leave an old man his pride," he said loudly enough for Jax to hear. "I scared myself and then I scared you. I'm sorry. I'm feeling much better now. You're like medicine, Nicole. I look at you and I see your mother and I remember my youth when I was strong and virile and had the whole future ahead of me." As he talked he opened wine and poured three glasses.

"Let's sit in the den. I want to know about your movie and the work, and then I want you to tell me all about this earring they say you stole."

Nicole handed Jax a glass of wine but couldn't meet his gaze. She wasn't used to talking about her personal business in front of anyone. Vincent didn't have that problem. He had always been open about his business, his ideas, his plans for the future. And now he was just as open about hers.

She watched as Jax took a seat directly across from her father. She took a chair between them at the small table.

"So, you're Nicole's boss? Tell me a little about yourself," Vincent said to Jax.

Nicole felt a warm flush begin to creep up her neck. She'd never had the experience of having her father grill one of her prospective dates. Vincent had been in prison throughout her entire teenage years. Now he was acting like Jax was her high school prom date.

Jax flashed Nicole a grin. "I'm from Texas," he said in his slow drawl, "and I coordinate the stunts on *Midnight Magic*."

"My daughter is beautiful, is she not?"

"Daddy!"

Jax only laughed. He seemed to be enjoying her father's company, though Nicole felt extremely uncomfortable.

"I have to admit, sir, that Nicole may be the most beautiful woman I've ever seen." Jax carefully avoided making eye contact with her.

"I can't believe this," she said. "I rush over here because I think my father's sick, and now the two of you gang up on me and try to embarrass me to death." She was outdone with both the men. And they were just sitting there, smiling at each other.

"I'm an old man," Vincent started out.

"Daddy, don't you dare start that old-man stuff. Whenever you do that, you're going to say something outrageous and then think you can get away with it because you pretend to be old. You're only sixty-two. That's not even old."

"I'm an old man," Vincent said again, ignoring everything Nicole had just said. "And my daughter's happiness is the most important thing to me."

"Daddy!"

"So I want to know what your relationship is to my daughter?"

"Good lord," Nicole said, putting her head down on her arms. "I think I just might die of shame."

"At the moment," Jax said, ignoring Nicole and staring Vincent right in the eyes, "I'm not sure what kind of relationship Nicole would be interested in."

"That's a dodge, young man," Vincent said with a sparkle in his eyes. "A clever one, but a dodge nonetheless."

"Daddy!" Nicole wanted to sink through the floor.

"Your daughter is one of the loveliest women I've ever met," Jax said, and this time his gaze lingered on Nicole. She felt as if her lungs had shrunk. "But I think she isn't a woman who would appreciate being pushed. So I'm going to have to decline to answer your question, Mr. Paul, because I think the only person who should answer it for you is Nicole. But I can tell you that I'd be very, very interested in hearing her answer."

Nicole found it nearly impossible to look away from Jax's intense gaze, but she dropped her gaze to the floor and took a deep breath. "Then both of you will just have to wait. I'm not prepared to give an answer. And that's the end of the discussion."

Chapter Four

"My parents were French immigrants," Vincent said as he poured more wine into Jax's glass. "My grandfather was one of the most prestigious jewelry makers in all of France, and my father was at the point in his career where he was poised to rival even my grandfather's talent. But then the war came. Our world of beauty was destroyed. My father moved my mother and me to the United States. He returned to France and was killed by the Germans."

Nicole held her untouched wine and listened. Her father had been ill before, but now he seemed perfectly recovered—and quite willing to tell Jax McClure the entire Paul family history. This was a story she normally loved to hear, but it made her nervous with Jax in the room. Vincent was too open, too free with details and emotions. She'd learned bitter lessons in how that could be turned against her family.

"How old were you when you emigrated?" Jax asked.

To all appearances, Jax seemed absorbed in the story. Nicole discreetly checked her watch. This saga had been going on for over an hour. And Jax kept asking questions. She wanted to drum her fingers on the table, but she didn't. Her father's face was aglow as he recalled anecdotes about his family and the jewelry shop they'd owned in Paris.

"I was an infant when we came to America. My father, Jean-Jacque, was becoming recognized as a master," Vincent said. "His work with stones was renowned. And before he died, he inspired me to follow in his footsteps."

"Now that you're free, are you going to resume your work?" Jax asked.

Nicole was suddenly tense. This was the question she hadn't been able to ask her father. Jewelry making had been everything to Vincent. After her mother had died, Vincent had focused totally on his work and his daughter. But after the horror of being accused of stealing, would Vincent be able to go back to the art he loved?

"I gather you know about my time in prison?" Vincent asked in that point-blank way.

"Very little," Jax said. "I heard you were unjustly accused of stealing a valuable diamond that was never found."

"Then you've heard the truth. I was creating a necklace for the jewel. It was the most exquisite stone I've ever seen. A rare lavender diamond. It was said to have belonged, at one time, to Cleopatra, brought from the mines of the Congo into the land of Egypt as a token of esteem for a beautiful woman."

"I've heard it called the Dream of Isis, and I've also heard that it's cursed," Jax said.

Nicole tried to catch his eye and give him a discreet signal to take the conversation in another direction. She'd never seen her father talk about the diamond without getting emotional, and he'd already been upset once that evening.

"Yes, I have finally come to believe the diamond is cursed, though I can't figure out why that curse would apply to me. I never owned it. I merely possessed it for a short time while I created a gold necklace to hold it. And what a necklace it was! I had just finished and set the stone. It was perfection."

"What happened, Vincent?" Jax asked.

"I think this conversation has gone on long enough," Nicole said, pushing back her chair. "All of that happened twenty years ago. It's time to let it go."

"No, I don't think it is," Jax said so firmly that Nicole sat back down in her chair. "I'd like to hear about the diamond."

"And *I* don't think it's *good for my father* to talk about it," Nicole said with emphasis.

"On the contrary," Vincent said, "I think it would be very good. Mr. McClure seems to be a bright young man. A man capable of understanding the truth. And there is always the possibility that somehow this diamond bears on your current dilemma, Nicole."

"How?" She rose. "What are you saying? That someone planted a stolen earring on me because of something that happened twenty years ago?'' This was exactly what she'd feared—that her father would somehow absorb the burden of guilt for what had happened to her.

Vincent put his hands on the table and stared at them. ''I haven't told you the complete truth about tonight,'' he said softly. ''I never would have called you, but I was afraid I was having another heart attack and I wanted to tell you how much I love you.'' He lifted a hand and laid it on top of hers. ''And I do love you, Nicole. You're the most beautiful of all the jewels in my life.''

She felt again the warm flush of embarrassment. Her father's effusive nature was sometimes too much. ''Oh, Daddy, just tell me what you're talking about.''

''I got a phone call tonight. Just before I called you. When I answered, a man said that you were a beautiful woman. There was something in his voice that terrified me. It was as if he were saying all of the horrible things he could do to you if he chose, but he never said any of them.''

Nicole found that her breathing was shallow. She took a deep breath and looked at Jax. He was totally focused on her father, listening intently.

''What did the man say exactly? Can you remember?'' Jax asked.

''Yes, I will remember these words to my grave. He said, 'The past is dragging behind you. Where is the Dream of Isis? Return it and nothing unpleasant will happen to those you love.'''

Vincent's face had grown pale again as he remembered the phone call that had so upset him. Nicole gathered his hand into hers and held on. His fingers were icy cold.

"Daddy, no one is going to hurt me. You don't have to worry."

"Did this man tell you how to get in touch with him?" Jax asked.

Vincent shook his head. "He said he'd call me back. He said he knew that I was sick, and that meant he'd have to act fast."

"Act fast?" Nicole repeated. She didn't like the sound of that at all. "Act fast how?"

Jax caught her gaze and held it. She didn't like what she saw in his eyes.

"Did he say anything else?" Jax pressed.

"No," Vincent said. "It was very fast. He called and before I could really think, he hung up. Then my blood pressure shot up and I thought I was going to die. That's when I called Nicole."

Jax leaned back in his chair. "Mr. Paul, this is truly none of my business, but I have to ask. Do you know where that jewel is?"

Vincent's smile was wan. "I have no idea. I told the truth when I was arrested. The diamond was in my workshop. I'd rented a space on Wilshire Boulevard, a lovely little shop with terrific window displays, and I'd acquired commissions to create jewelry for four of the five actresses nominated for an Oscar that year. It was to be the year that launched

Vincent Paul as the hottest jewelry designer in this country. I was bringing my family's reputation from France to this new world of opportunity." There was a long pause. "And what happened is that I went to jail."

Nicole found herself blinking back tears. Her father's loss was so acute she felt it intensely. Looking at Jax, she saw that he, too, was moved by her father's grief.

"Mr. Paul," Jax said, "I know this may be upsetting, but can you tell me what happened when the diamond was stolen."

"Of course. As I said, I'd just set the stone in the gold necklace I'd prepared for it. Monica Kane was supposed to retrieve the necklace the next morning. She was having her gown fitted and needed the necklace to be sure it draped properly, putting the focus on the jewel. All odds were on that Monica would win the Oscar for best actress for her role in *Sundown Sonata*."

"Had you finished the jewelry for the other actresses, too?"

Vincent frowned. "I had earrings to make for Julie Lansing, and after that I was done."

"Were those jewels still in your shop?"

"Most of them were gone. But there were many other valuable stones there. Some set, others unset."

"And what was taken?"

"Only the Dream of Isis." Vincent's voice was low. "That one stone. The one that ruined me. I could have replaced the others, made amends. But that one was irreplaceable.''

"How did the thief get in?"

Vincent lifted his eyebrows. "A mystery. The high-tech security systems of today weren't available. I had a system wired to the nearest police precinct. The alarm was never tripped. The back door was forced open, but the police found only my fingerprints there.''

"It's a strange case," Jax said. "And there's been no sign of the diamond since?''

"None. It simply vanished.''

"Would someone who loved jewelry want it badly enough to take it and then never be able to wear it or display it?''

Vincent thought. ''Most people want to show off their jewelry. Owning it is a matter of pride. But there are those rare collectors who hoard their possessions. Their desire is to hide them from the world, to retain the pleasure of looking at them only for themselves. I don't understand this, but I know it is true.''

"I don't understand it either, but I've seen it," Jax agreed. ''And what was the evidence against you at the trial?''

"The stone was in my possession. Then it was gone.'' He shrugged his shoulders. ''There was no sign of another person in the store. The diamond had been left in my safe, which was opened with the correct combination.''

"Did anyone else know the combination?" Jax asked.

"No one," Vincent said.

Jax nodded. "And this man who called tonight, did you recognize his voice?"

"No, he sounded much younger than I am. He sounded tough and capable of hurting Nicole." He reached out for his daughter and drew her against his side. "I'm not afraid for myself. But for Nicole…" He didn't finish the sentence.

"I'm fine, Dad. Really fine. And I'm in top physical shape."

"She is that," Jax said reassuringly. "Nicole can handle herself, sir. I promise you that."

"I realize it's hard to believe, Mr. McClure, but there was a time when I could also handle myself. Twenty years in prison takes a lot of the starch out of a man."

"We have to go, Daddy. If anyone calls you again, simply hang up. Then call me. I'll think of something to do about this. Maybe we should call the police."

Vincent shook his head. "No police. You forget, Nicole, that I'm a convicted felon. My version of events will never be believed."

"But someone is threatening you!"

"No, they're threatening you. And it would seem that he made good on his threat. You spent the afternoon in jail, didn't you? Accused of the exact thing that I was convicted of, only to a lesser degree. And those charges still hang over you."

"I agree with you, Mr. Paul. I think this incident

with Nicole is directly related to the Dream of Isis. And I also believe that we should keep the police out of this. If anyone is going to really solve it, it's going to have to be us.''

Nicole looked at Jax. Really looked at him. He had jumped into the snarl of their lives with both feet. Any other man would be running in the opposite direction.

''Why are you doing this?'' Nicole asked him, deciding that sometimes her father's blunt approach was the best.

''I believe your father lost twenty years of his life for a crime he didn't commit. I don't believe you stole Angela's earring. It looks like history is trying to repeat itself, unless someone stops it.''

''And that someone is you?'' Vincent asked, a glint in his eyes. ''This is a man of ethics and action, Nicole. I think he has potential.''

She felt again the burn of embarrassment. ''We aren't buying him, Dad.''

''No, perhaps not. But let me just say, Mr. Mc-Clure, that if you keep my daughter safe, I will consider a very handsome dowry for the man who can make her happy.''

''Daddy!'' Nicole was mortified, but both men were chuckling.

''It's a joke, Nicole,'' Vincent said, still laughing. ''Mr. McClure doesn't take me seriously.''

''I don't,'' Jax agreed, his gaze lingering on Nicole in a way that made her skin hot. What ideas was Vincent planting in the man's head?

He moved to stand beside Nicole, his hand lightly touching her elbow. "It's been a pleasure, Mr. Paul. Thank you for talking to me so honestly. I have some ideas, and as soon as I have any new information for you, I'll be in touch."

Nicole kissed her father's cheek and walked into the April night with Jax.

"I apologize for my father. He's lost twenty years in jail. I don't think he always understands how much our society has changed."

"It hasn't changed that much, Nicole," Jax said in his slow drawl. "Back in Texas, some of the society gals still let their daddies arrange a marriage for them. It guarantees a certain standard in life."

"That is repugnant," Nicole snapped. "The idea that someone would have to arrange a marriage or pay some man to marry his daughter—it's atrocious."

Jax handed her a helmet. He straddled the bike and held it as she swung a leg over. She was still adjusting her seat when she felt him turn.

"How much would your father consider to be a reasonable dowry?" Jax asked just before he turned the key and sent the motorcycle down the hair-raising driveway.

Nicole had no response. She had her hands full hanging on to Jax's narrow waist. But she knew her moment would come when she'd be able to repay him for his teasing. And it would be sweet revenge.

I WONDER WHERE Nicole has gone. Jax's motorcycle is gone, too. I turn my back for one moment, and the two of them are out of here like they're shot from a cannon. My little kitty instinct tells me they're together. That is some consolation. Felines are solitary creatures. Humanoids are more canine. They like to run in packs. Rather clumsy in some instances, but it does keep them out of a lot of trouble.

Especially someone like Nicole. She's used to handling things on her own, but this is one time she's going to need all the help she can get. Moi, for example, and the hunky cowboy stuntman. I have to say, of all the guys on the set here, Jax is the man I'd most want to cover my back.

I've been lurking around the movie set and I've learned some very interesting things. Such as the fact that Nicole's phone has been ringing off the hook. I can't wait for her to get home and ease my curiosity.

Even more interesting was the surprise visit by world famous actress Monica Kane. She's in her late forties and still as voluptuous as ever. Va-va-voom! I could get into a little lap time with her.

I was so starstruck I couldn't help but sneak over to eavesdrop on her conversation with John Hudson. It seems that Monica is going to do a guest appearance in this film. Just a little cameo role because the actress John had originally signed on has come down with some liver ailment.

Monica and John must be old friends from way back. They certainly seemed glad to see each other. I guess that's mostly true when two complementary talents meet. Monica is acclaimed for her dramatic roles, but she hasn't done a lot of comedy. This will stretch her skills and perhaps open new doors for her. Unfortunately, a lot of the old doors—romantic lead, leading lady, femme fatale—are closing.

It's a crummy business when a woman has to begin to look for feature roles in her forties. Monica is still one hot lady, but she's smart enough to see the handwriting on the wall. If she doesn't show her willingness to step down from the leading lady slot, she won't work. The romantic leads go to the twentysomethings and the thirtysomethings, like that witch Angela Myers. The fortysomethings get to play beauticians, waitresses and loving mothers. It just ain't fair.

But the most interesting aspect of Monica's appearance is that she's playing such a small role. I think John Hudson was shocked that she accepted the part. I can't help but wonder if there isn't something else going on. Something to do with Nicole.

In this film, Monica is going to play a rich actress who is burglarized by the heroine and the cat. That would be Angela and Elvis on the screen credits, but it will actually be me and Nicole doing all of the work. Another of Hollywood's grand illusions. But now isn't the time for philosophy or whining, I'll get on with my story.

Monica and John were talking about how many days it would take to shoot her part and that kind of thing when Monica asked if it was true that Vincent Paul's daughter was on the set and if she, too, had been accused of stealing something.

Monica knew all about Nicole's father. I was just surprised that news of Nicole's arrest had already left the set. But I shouldn't be surprised. Gossip flies faster than anything else in the world. I didn't learn anything of any significance, but it was just odd that Monica would bring up Nicole's name. Odd because I don't know the background here. But by tomorrow afternoon, I'll be well-versed in past history.

I've been hanging around three hours, waiting for Nicole so I could try and fill her in on what I know, but I'm not certain she's coming home tonight. Too bad. It's always difficult at first to establish that link with a new humanoid, and with the schedule of filming, I don't have a lot of time alone with Nicole.

I wish Eleanor and Peter weren't so busy. I'd get them to help me talk to Nicole. They're terribly good at translating from cat to human. Then again, if they weren't so busy, I wouldn't be able to roam about at night. They like to keep me under wraps and out of trouble as much as possible. That never works, but God bless their hearts, they just keep trying.

It looks as if Nicole is out for the night. I don't know why I never considered that she might have a boyfriend. That's the most likely explanation for the fact that here's her car and there's no sign of her in her trailer. I doubt she walked anywhere. This movie set is on the backside of nowhere. So she obviously caught a ride with someone.

Should I be worried? It just seems hard to really worry about Nicole. She's so physically competent. I mean she scaled that three-story house like it was a sand hill. I was most impressed.

And if I'm any judge at all, I think Jax McClure was equally impressed. The way he was watching Nicole was very interesting. I get the impression Jax is a man who doesn't believe he's vulnerable to a woman's charms. He's one of those tough guys who believe he's had his last romantic bronc ride. Well, I do believe he's getting ready to learn differently.

All I can say is, "Cowboy up!"

Chapter Five

Jax lay on the bed. A gentle breeze blew the gossamer curtains at the windows, billowing them in and out, creating the shape of a woman in their folds, then making her disappear. The undulating curtains made him eager for the woman he knew was only a few feet away. Smiling, Jax watched as Nicole stepped into the bedroom from the moonlit balcony outside.

"Nicole," he whispered. The moonlight struck her blond hair, gilding it as it fell over her bare breasts. He'd never seen a vision more lovely. "Nicole!" He held out his hand to her and she came toward him, her dark gaze locked on to his.

Her hand was warm and soft and he felt it glide over his cheek. His own hands grasped her firm, lithe body, lifting her gently as he helped her into bed with him.

He wanted to kiss her. His desire was uncontrollable. But Nicole laughed softly, avoiding his kiss as her hands moved over his body, following the contours of his muscles.

He groaned and tightened his hold on her slim waist. She was muscular and toned, a woman who worked at keeping herself fit. He tried to rise up on his elbow so that she was beneath him.

Laughing, Nicole evaded him.

Jax heard himself moan again. He'd never met a woman more exciting, more desirable, yet she was also a sweet torment. She was playing with him and enjoying every minute of it. That was the danger. A woman like Nicole, once she learned her power, couldn't help but exert it. And down that road lay ruin.

Even as he let those thoughts into his mind he felt Nicole begin to slip away from him. He felt for her in the tangled sheets but she wasn't there. The mattress where she'd lain was still warm, but there was no other sign of her.

He heard her footfalls receding, a gentle pounding as she left him.

"Nicole!" *he called softly.* "Don't go."

"Jax!"

The voice calling his name was definitely not Nicole's, nor was it very comforting.

"Jax! What in the hell are you doing in there?"

Jax forced his eyes open. The first thing he did was check the bedside clock. It was after nine. Instinctively he jumped to his feet. He looked around, confused. The dream had been so intense. Now he was simply in the bedroom of his trailer. There was no moonlit balcony, no billowing curtains.

And no Nicole.

Man, he had really been deep, deep in dreamland.

"Jax, man, if you don't open the door I'm going to bust it down. You sounded like you were dying!"

Jax recognized the real concern in Jason's voice. "I'm okay," he said. "Bad dream." But was it really a bad dream? He thought about it. Bad and good. As a vague image of Nicole slipping out of the curtains, her naked body glowing, came back to him, he had to admit that the dream was deliciously good on one level. His hands could still recall the feel of her firm flesh, the dip of her waist. The surge of desire was like a rush of adrenaline.

Even when he was wide-awake the dream had the power to move him.

He found a pair of jeans and slipped into them, picking up his boots and a cotton shirt as he left his room. Jason was standing in the small kitchen of the trailer eating a banana and drinking a protein shake.

"What's going on?" Jason asked. "You sounded desperate. You were moaning like you'd been beaten half to death. What were you dreaming about?"

Jax gave a crooked grin. "If I told you, I'd have to kill you," he jested.

"Okay, lover boy, keep your secrets," Jason said, downing the last of his shake. "I thought you might show up at the bar after the poker game. Marla and I missed you."

"I had something else to do," Jax said, pouring a cup of coffee. He liked Marla and admired the fact that she'd lassoed Jason—and managed to hold him.

"Would that something have anything to do with Nicole?"

Jax sipped his coffee. He and Jason had an easy, comfortable friendship. They'd worked together on several movies before this one, and he knew Jason to be more than competent at his job and always reliable. Still, he felt a real reluctance to reveal anything about Nicole. "I'm supposed to check that climbing harness. Can you give me a hand?"

Jason rinsed out his glass and put it in the sink. "Nicole must either be extremely hot or extremely cold." He grinned. "She's a beauty. Too bad she isn't all that friendly. I think she'd like my girlfriend Marla if she gave it a try. Anyway, rough break about that earring. Did she say how it got in her trailer?"

"Nicole isn't a good topic," Jax said. He'd hoped to dissuade Jason gently but decided to tackle the situation head-on.

Jason nodded. "Gotcha. Sorry, Jax. I didn't mean to pry. Did you hear that Monica Kane is on the set today?"

Jax was surprised. "Really?"

"She's replacing Kim Lumet. It's a shame about Kim's illness. Anyway, John called Monica yesterday and she agreed to step in."

"I'm surprised," Jax said, and in more ways than one. In a twenty-four hour period, three separate incidents had occurred that provided a link to the theft of the Dream of Isis. Jax wasn't certain what was going on, but he had a gut feeling that it was more than coincidence at work.

"Oh, yeah, that girl they hired as the waitress can't make the shoot either. John was furious. Now he may have to shut down production this afternoon because he doesn't have someone to stand behind a cash register and say, 'Can I help you, ma'am?'"

"He shouldn't have any trouble finding another bit player."

"It's the timing that had him upset. He's due to shoot that scene this afternoon. The crew's already lit the set."

"You have to admit, this is a crazy business." Jax finished his coffee and stood up, stretching. He did feel as if he hadn't gotten a wink of sleep. It was going to be a long, arduous day. He could only wonder how Nicole was feeling. When he'd dropped her off at her trailer, she'd looked emotionally drained.

Jason put his banana peel in the garbage can. "We have to be on the set in three minutes. I hope it doesn't matter that you need a shave and look like hell." He gave Jax a slap on the shoulder and was whistling as he left the trailer.

NICOLE OPENED ONE EYE and saw the blinking light on her answering machine. She reached one long arm over and punched the replay button.

"Nicole, Ms. Paul, please pick up. This is Connie. Remember me? You gave me this number. Please pick up." There was the sound of sobbing.

Nicole sat up in bed, instantly awake.

"My boyfriend dropped the charges and he got me out of jail. I had to go with him. I didn't have anywhere else to go. But he told me he was going to make me pay. When he stopped at a red light, I got out and ran. Now I'm at a pay phone and I don't know what to do. I just want to go home to Arkansas. This city is too hard. I just want to go home.'' There was more sobbing.

Nicole listened for a phone number, but there was nothing else. She replayed her entire message, counting nine hang-up calls. Those were probably Connie, she realized, too afraid to say anything. Desperation had finally pushed her into revealing her plight.

But there was no number and no way to contact the young girl. Nicole sat down on the bed, dejected at the idea that she hadn't been available to help Connie when the girl needed her.

She heard a soft scratching on the door of her trailer. Puzzled, she got up and opened the door a crack. The golden gaze of the cat looked up at her.

''Familiar,'' she said, opening the door wide. ''We're not due to shoot a scene until this afternoon.''

''Meow,'' the cat said, moving past her. She followed him to the telephone. In a moment he was at the answering machine, patting the buttons as if he understood how it worked.

Curious, Nicole replayed the messages. Familiar sat on her bed, his head tilted. When the message was finished, he knocked the telephone out of its cradle. With one delicate black paw he punched *69. Nicole heard the phone ringing and she was amazed when a young girl answered the phone.

"Connie?" she asked hopefully.

"Who is this?" The young voice was scared, desperate.

"This is Nicole Paul. I'm looking for Connie." She almost cursed. She didn't even know the girl's last name.

"Nicole!" The relief was intense. "How did you know to call me at this phone?"

Nicole looked at the black cat. "I had a little help from a very smart feline. Where are you?"

Connie gave the street address. "I was so upset last night. I hid in the phone booth, and I guess I finally fell asleep."

"My car is on the fritz," Nicole said. "I want you to get a cab and come on out here." She gave the street address.

"That's going to cost a fortune. I don't have any money," Connie said.

"It's okay," Nicole assured her, reaching across the room and finding her purse. She dug through it until she had her billfold. Opening it up, she counted out four twenties. Surely that would cover the taxi ride. "Don't worry about the money. I'll take care of it."

"I don't know what else to do," Connie said. "Kevin told me he was going to make me really sorry."

"Don't even think about him." Nicole was no authority on abusive relationships, but she knew enough to realize that Connie had to get away from her boyfriend before he seriously hurt her.

"Okay. I can get a cab. Are you sure?"

"Positive. I'll be waiting for you at the security gate with the money for the taxi."

"I don't know why you're doing this, but I can't thank you enough. If I can just get some work to earn enough money to go home, I'm headed back to Arkansas."

JAX FINISHED SETTING up the stunt, making sure that Elvis the black cat was stage left, ready for his entrance. The scene involved Angela's character going through the loot she and Elvis had just stolen from a wealthy man who loved his money and jewelry more than his wife and family.

Angela was supposed to hold up some of the jewels and admire them as Elvis jumped on her lap. Then someone would shoot through the window, and Elvis would save Angela by pushing her out of the way.

The scene had been rehearsed numerous times, against the protests of Angela, who made no secret of the fact that she found the cat to be dirty and unsanitary. Such animosity had grown between the star and the cat that Jax wondered if they'd be able to complete the film. He had to agree with the cat— Angela was insufferable.

And John Hudson's temper, while legendary at best, was at the point of a powder keg. Jason was right. The failure of a bit actress to show up for her part had put a real dent in John's production schedule. The shooting was already tight, mainly due to Angela's demands. Jax wiped his forehead on the sleeve of his shirt.

"I'm ready," he said, nodding to Elvis's trainer. Peter and Eleanor Curry stood well out of the way, watching the cat's behavior, offering comments whenever they saw something that might be improved. Jax was glad for their help.

"Camera! Action!"

Angela picked up the jewels and held them up, turning them so the light picked up their hue and beauty. "You'll be back with your owner as soon as he shows proper appreciation for the beauty of his family," Angela said.

Elvis made his entrance into the scene, strutting with great confidence. He leaped into Angela's lap, one paw going up to stroke a necklace as if to admire it, too.

"We make quite a team, don't we?" Angela said to the cat.

As Jax watched, he was amazed at how much Angela seemed to like the cat. She was a better actress than he'd given her credit for. On screen, she came across as the cat's most devoted fan. In reality, she'd have had Elvis tied in a sack and thrown in the river if she thought she could get away with it.

"Cut and print!" John said, standing up from his chair. "At last we get a scene on the first try. At last."

He strode toward Jax. Jax saw him coming and checked the scene list. The next slated scene was in the diner with the waitress, but since the actress hadn't shown up, he figured they'd skip on to the next scene.

"Mr. Hudson!"

Jax recognized Nicole's voice and turned to find her striding across the parking lot with a teenage girl following her like a puppy.

"I heard we lost the waitress. I found someone who may be able to replace her."

"Replace her?" John sounded frosty. "I didn't realize you were a casting agency now?"

Nicole stopped so suddenly the young girl ran into her back. "I'm sorry. I didn't mean to presume. I was only trying to help."

John's coldness thawed a little. "Is this the girl?" he asked, signaling the redhead to step out from behind Nicole.

"Yes, sir," Nicole said, tugging Connie forward. "This is Connie King. She's an actress from Arkansas."

"And you've worked in films before?" John asked.

Connie stammered, swallowed, and stammered again. Finally she spoke. "Are you really John Hudson? *The* John Hudson." She trembled so much that she visible shook.

"Yes, I'm John Hudson, obviously a figure of great terror to you."

"Oh, no sir, I'm not afraid. It's just that I never dreamed I'd really meet you. I've seen all of your films. *Memphis on a Raft* was my favorite, but I liked them all.''

In the face of such unmitigated worship, John thawed even more. ''So, you've acted before, young lady?''

''In my high school plays. I got all the leads. I—''

''High school?'' he said, frowning at Nicole. ''I don't have time for this. I need a professional.''

''Give her a chance,'' Nicole pleaded. ''Just let her try it. It's the next scene. Everything is set up. What could it hurt?''

John looked down at the shooting script in his hand. ''It would really help us out to get this scene finished and move on. This is the last one in the diner. We could dismantle it.'' He looked at Connie. ''You look right for the part. Okay, one try. But I'm not wasting my time trying to teach some young woman to act.''

''Oh, no sir, I can act. You just have to tell me what you want. I haven't had a chance to read the script so I don't know my character.''

''She's a waitress. High school dropout. She loves cats, especially black ones, and she is madly in love with a young mechanic who comes into the café. But she's too shy to tell him she's interested, and he's too poor to show an interest in her.''

''Oh, heck, I don't even have to act to do that one,'' Connie said with a glimmer of self-confidence. ''That sounds just like my best friend Kiley, back in Arkansas. She married George against everybody's advice and they're as happy as pigs in mud.''

"Pigs in mud," John said to a hovering assistant, "write that into the script. It gives the character a real flavor."

In a few moments Connie was dressed in the aqua waitress uniform that showed off her trim waist and well-shaped legs. She stood behind the counter, a pencil behind her ear. She'd been coached on her one line and she was ready to go.

From the sidelines Nicole watched the scene with real pride. Connie was no longer the timid mouse. Now that she was in character she was wiping the counter, swaying her hips, plucking a bit of meringue off a slice of chocolate pie and licking her finger.

"My God, she's a natural," John said loud enough for all of the camera crew to hear.

The scene ended and everyone in the area began to applaud.

Connie beamed. "This is just as wonderful as I thought it would be. I've dreamed about this moment my entire life. This is all I ever wanted, and at least I got to do it one time before I had to go back home to Arkansas."

"Home to Arkansas?" John asked. "Why are you leaving town?"

"I sort of got myself in a mess," Connie admitted, some of the self-confidence falling from her face. "I fell in with the wrong sort of man. That's how I got arrested."

"Arrested?" John turned to Nicole. "This young child has a criminal record?"

"No, the charges were dropped," Nicole said,

aware that everyone on the crew was now looking at her. She'd never expected Connie to blurt out everything about her past. In some ways, Connie was a lot like her father. They just told every gritty detail.

"How would you like another scene?" John asked Connie.

"Another one? For real? I'd pay *you* to let me do it!"

The laughter was so loud that Connie flushed red. "I guess that didn't sound very professional, did it?"

"It was charming," John said, all frostiness gone and replaced with a warm smile. "I think I've just expanded your part in the movie. That is if you can hold off on going back to Arkansas."

"I can hold off real fine," Connie said, grinning. "I can hold off forever if I get a chance to act."

Nicole couldn't help smiling at Connie's youth and enthusiasm. She felt someone behind her and was suddenly aware of Jax. He hadn't touched her or spoken her name, but she knew he was there.

"Have you heard about Monica?" he asked.

"I heard she was coming onto the set."

"I find that a little more than coincidental," Jax said.

"So did I."

"Let's meet at four, at the concession. We need to talk, but I don't want to be obvious about it."

"I'll be there," Nicole promised.

Chapter Six

Walking into the break area, Nicole immediately saw Jax. He was sitting at a table, two bottles of water in front of him. Slouched back in the chair, he looked like every woman's fantasy of a cowboy. His jeans, worn and faded, clung to slim hips and long, powerful legs. The white snap-button shirt was immaculate, but looked as if it had been washed a thousand times. And the cowboy hat he wore was straw, crimped just a little on the brim to prove it had hit the dirt often—just like the stuntman who wore it.

The flutter in Nicole's stomach alerted her to the fact that she was nervous about this meeting. She'd finished her scenes earlier and had taken time for a hot shower and a change of wardrobe. Red shorts and a white pullover replaced the black cat suit she'd worn in the stunt. She'd even painted her toenails and put on her sandals. Summer was just around the corner in California.

As she started to move forward, she felt his gaze touch her and then lock on. The look in his blue eyes made her feel first cold and then hot. He was looking at her like a predator. A hungry one, at that. But when she got close enough, he smiled. The hungry look disappeared, replaced by one of pleasure.

"Jax," she said, taking the seat he pointed out. "I hope you weren't waiting long."

He handed her a bottle of water. "I considered a fudge brownie with ice cream, but then I remembered I'm going to have to haul you out of a gully tomorrow. Got to look out for my back, you know."

Before he could finish speaking, he let out a sharp yelp and ducked down under the table. Curious, Nicole also ducked down. Familiar was under the table, and he had two front paws hooked into Jax's shin. Nicole sat back up, a smile on her face.

"What does he want?" Jax asked, his voice strained. "He's tearing the flesh from my shin."

"He wants you to be nice to me," she said sweetly. "Another comment about my weight and you'll be headed to the hospital for a skin graft."

"It was only a joke," Jax apologized. "Eat the whole pan of brownies and five gallons of ice cream. You'll still be lithe and lovely."

Nicole realized Familiar had released Jax's leg when she felt the black cat jump in her lap. He wasted no time hopping on top of the table. In a moment he'd knocked down the menu and was tapping it impatiently.

"What does he want now?" Jax asked, a little wary of the cat.

"Ice cream?" Nicole hazarded, looking at the picture.

"We'll take care of that order right away."

As soon as he spoke, the cat sat down and began to groom himself, perfectly content.

"Jax, last night you were asking me about my dowry, remember?" She lifted one eyebrow. "I dare you to ask that question again with Familiar here."

"As if the cat could truly understand—yow!" He froze, one hand on the table pinned beneath Familiar's big black paw. Familiar's claws were extended just enough to hang in the skin. "Tell the cat to remove his claws. I won't ever tease you about your weight and I'll never mention the word *dowry* again."

"Familiar," Nicole said sweetly. "He's given up. You can let him go now and order whatever you'd like. He's treating you."

The black cat returned to the menu, and in a moment his paw settled on a grilled shrimp basket.

"Anything else?" Jax asked sarcastically. He looked at Nicole. "This is amazing. I've worked with a lot of animals, but how did you teach him to do all of this?"

"I didn't," Nicole said. "I told you he was special, that he was a private investigator. And he is. He can also let you know exactly what he wants when he wants it."

"He doesn't have a problem making his wishes known," Jax agreed, placing the cat's order. "Anything you'd like, Nicole?"

Nicole considered. "That brownie does sound awfully good."

"And two brownies with vanilla ice cream and fudge sauce," Jax told the waitress.

Once their order was in, Jax looked around the area. Because the movie was being filmed in a small valley outside Los Angles, the concession was outdoors. About a dozen tables with umbrellas had been set up, and Jax made sure no one was close enough to overhear their conversation.

"Have you seen Monica Kane?" Jax asked.

Nicole was about to answer when the cat perked up. He put a paw on her chin.

"What?" She knew Familiar was extremely smart, but sometimes she had trouble figuring out what he was trying to tell her.

Familiar meowed softly and looked over her shoulder.

"He's letting you know Monica Kane is about ten feet behind you," Jax said in a whisper.

Nicole felt her heart begin to pound. It had been twenty years since she'd last met Monica face-to-face. And the last scene had been ugly. Monica had come into the jewelry shop and demanded that Vincent return the diamond. Nicole had been behind the counter of the shop. The media lingered outside like vultures, hoping for just such a scene as the one Monica seemed determined to provide for them.

Vincent had tried to tell her that he didn't have the diamond, but she'd railed at him. The Dream of Isis had been loaned to her by a personal friend. She'd guaranteed the security of the stone. And now it was gone and she was left looking like a fool.

And when Vincent had tried once again to tell Monica of his innocence, she'd slapped him and stalked out of the shop. A film crew had caught the entire scene on tape and played it on the six o'clock news. It had also been used by the prosecution in the high-drama trial.

Nicole didn't turn around, but she could read the expression on Jax's face as Monica approached her. Nicole steeled herself for whatever the woman had to dish out.

"Nicole," Monica said in a sugary voice. "I haven't seen you since you were a child, but I'd recognize you anywhere."

Nicole saw the wariness in Jax's eyes and the narrowing of Familiar's. She turned slowly to face the brunette beauty.

"Monica," she said, "it has been a long time. Twenty years. It was in the courtroom of my father's trial, wasn't it?"

Monica's eyebrows drew together. "I suppose so. I don't like to dwell on those days. But I hear Vincent is out of prison now. I believe the judge would have been more lenient on him if he'd simply given up the stone. I wonder if it's worth the loss of twenty years?"

Nicole rose very slowly and turned to face Monica. "My father never stole the diamond. He doesn't know where it is. No stone is worth the price he had to pay."

Monica smiled. "You look a lot like him when you're angry, dear. I find your loyalty quite impressive. But you were only a child when all of this happened. You know only the details your father told you."

"We'd love to hear your version of the event," Jax said, also rising. "Join us, Ms. Kane."

"And who are you?" Monica asked, turning coy.

"Jax McClure, stunt coordinator. And this is Familiar, the stunt cat."

"How clever, an introduction to a cat," Monica trilled as she took the seat Jax pulled out for her.

Nicole was ready to spit nails. The last thing she wanted was to sit down and talk to Monica Kane. More likely she'd prefer pulling her hair out—carefully dyed hair, she was quick to notice. And Monica's "ageless beauty" was showing the first signs of wear, though Nicole had to admit she looked superb in her white linen suit.

"Tell us what you think happened to the Dream of Isis," Jax prodded Monica.

Under the table, Nicole felt Jax's foot rub against hers. It was a small signal for her to keep her cool, to listen, to use this as an opportunity to figure out what may have happened in the past. She didn't like it, but she realized that Jax was acting in her best interest.

"It was such a long time ago," Monica said, shaking her head. "It was my moment to shine, and I lost it because of…" She glanced at Nicole. "Well, because that diamond was stolen."

"I was on a cattle farm in Texas when all of this

took place, so I don't know the gritty details. Who did the diamond belong to?'' Jax asked.

"What difference does that make?'' Monica snapped. "I was the one responsible for it. I was the one who suffered.''

"But who owned it?'' Jax insisted.

"A friend of mine. A Realtor named Richard Weeks. He'd just bought the stone at an auction in France and he said it would be the perfect adornment for me when I won the Oscar. The stone perfectly matched my eyes.''

Nicole couldn't help but roll her eyes at Familiar. The cat nodded.

"I'm sure that Mr. Weeks had the stone insured,'' Jax said.

"Yes, he did. But the value of the stone wasn't monetary. It was one-of-a-kind. It was magnificent. Money couldn't replace the loss.''

"No, but it would go a long way toward soothing the loss,'' Jax said. "And Mr. Weeks never received a ransom note or anything that might have indicated that someone had taken the stone for monetary gain?''

Monica paused. "Richard would have told me if someone had tried to ransom the stone. He never said a word. The stone simply vanished. That's why everyone believed that Vincent took it.''

"But how would it benefit Vincent?'' Jax asked her. "He can never show the stone. What good is it to him?''

Monica hesitated. She looked at Jax and then at

Nicole. "He can do anything he wants to now. He's served his time."

"That isn't true," Nicole said. "He didn't steal the diamond, and even if he had, he couldn't simply bring it out of hiding. Whoever has it, it still belongs to Richard Weeks."

A frown marred Monica's perfect forehead. "This is giving me a headache. I can't begin to fathom why Vincent would have done such a thing. I mean his artistry was about to be displayed at the Oscars. It was foolish of him to steal the diamond the night before."

"You're making my point for me," Jax said softly. "Think about it, Ms. Kane. It doesn't make any sense."

The waitress brought their orders. She placed the brownies and ice cream in front of Jax and Nicole and the shrimp basket on the table in front of Familiar.

"You're going to let that cat eat on the table with you?" Monica asked, making a face. "I heard Angela was complaining about having to work with a cat. She said she had fur all over her clothes every time the cat came within an inch of her. Ick!"

"Ms. Kane," Jax said, drawing her attention back to the conversation. "Did you know of anyone who might want the diamond for a private collection?"

"Of course not. If I'd known such a person, I would have said so."

"But you are willing to concede that it wouldn't

have been in Vincent's best interest to steal the diamond *before* the Oscars?'' Jax asked.

''I'm not willing to concede anything,'' Monica said. ''And this conversation is boring me.''

Just as she started to rise, Familiar tumbled on the table. It seemed he'd lost his balance and was about to fall. Instead, he kicked the heaping bowl of brownie, ice cream, and fudge sauce and sent it flying across the table and into Monica's white linen lap.

''Oh-oh-oh!'' Monica screamed as she scooted her chair back. ''You vile creature!'' she screeched at Familiar. ''You stupid cat!''

Nicole found that she could barely contain her laughter, and out of the corner of her eye, she caught Jax fighting to keep from smiling.

''Ms. Kane, I'm terribly sorry,'' Jax said, holding out his napkin to her. ''Familiar is seldom so clumsy. I think he must have been stung by something. Perhaps a bee.''

Monica wiped at the huge brown smear on her suit. ''This is ruined. This is an Eva Pilet original. Do you have any idea what this cost? Probably more than you make in a year.''

''Probably so,'' Jax said silkily. ''What a terrible accident.''

People at other tables had gotten up to take a look at the action. Monica turned around, confronting them. ''The show is over, and I promise all of you that cat is going to pay.'' She stormed out of the concession area.

Jax signaled the waitress, who walked up with a big grin. "We'd like another brownie and ice cream, double fudge sauce, and whenever the cat shows up here and wants something, put it on my tab."

Nicole was still fighting to contain her mirth when she locked her gaze with Jax. "What are you thinking?" she asked.

"I guess the more I think about it, the less sense it makes that your father would take that jewel the night before the Oscars."

"He didn't." .

"Monica was very helpful," he said, "even though she wasn't trying to be. I think a little visit to Richard Weeks is in order. Are you game?"

"Sure, but we have to shoot that ravine scene this evening." Nicole bit her bottom lip. This was one scene that gave her serious misgivings. Jax himself had rigged and checked that both harnesses would hold them over the canyon. Still, the script called for Nicole to swing like a pendulum until she could grab onto the rock wall of the canyon. According to the movie script, this was the place where she'd stashed the jewels she'd stolen.

She was to retrieve the jewels—just before someone started shooting at her.

"I'll see if I can get a number on this Richard Weeks character and set up an appointment for tomorrow. About five? Then maybe we could have dinner?"

Nicole felt a sudden tightening of her chest, and it

had nothing to do with the movie. Jax was asking her out on a date.

"I'd like that," she said. She found she was held by his blue gaze. "I'd like that a lot, Jax."

"Good. I'll see what I can do about setting it up. Now I have to go. I'll meet you in an hour at the ravine. Do you need a ride?"

She shook her head. "Connie looked at my car. The spark plug wires were loose. She fixed them. She's going to give me a ride over and then use the car to run an errand."

"Good," Jax said. "Where's she staying?"

"With me," Nicole admitted. "She doesn't really have any other place to go, and since John is going to use her in another scene…"

"You've got a tender heart, Nicole. And an eye for talent. Connie has real potential. Almost as much as you."

Nicole laughed, but she found that she was basking in Jax's praise. "See you in an hour," she said as she ate the last bite of her brownie and got up.

She looked around for Familiar, but the black cat had cleaned up his shrimp and was gone.

I SUPPOSE THAT WITCH Monica Kane would put a bounty on my head if she could, but I think I'm safe here. Just a little disappointed. I always liked Monica Kane. I enjoyed her in every role she's ever played. And now I discover that beneath that beautiful veneer is just another mean humanoid. Puts a whole new meaning on that old saw "Don't judge a book by its cover."

Nicole and Jax have work this evening. I'm off, thank goodness. I feel a need to dig a little deeper into the past. The question is how? How can I find what I need to know? I don't exactly have access to a library here. Or even a computer.

Hey, wait a minute. The cinematographer, O. J. Adams, had a real fancy setup. He does a lot of digital stuff, and I'm sure he's hooked up online. It would be simple enough to dig into a few archives.

I happen to understand he's a regular at the late-night poker games. That should make it a simple matter for me to visit his trailer and use his equipment.

For now, though, I'm going to spend a little lap time with my Eleanor. She was looking for me earlier and I didn't have time to respond to her. I could use a few kitty cuddles, my nice soft pillow, a nap and just a little attention focused only at me.

There's another question that's been nagging at me, too. Most of the focus has been put on Vincent Paul's innocence. But why would Angela Myers want to deliberately set Nicole up as a thief? Why? It just doesn't make sense. Maybe she doesn't like Nicole. Maybe she's intimidated by Nicole. All of that is well and good, but it doesn't answer the why question.

What would Angela gain by this? That's something else I intend to address.

Oh, look, there's Eleanor. She's trying to be blustery and act angry that I've been gone all day, but she's relenting. Look, she's making me a little snack *of fresh tuna. Yum. The shrimp were surprisingly good, but there's nothing like home cooking.*

Now I'm full and ready for a little nap. Wonderful, Eleanor's putting my pillow in the sun. Ah, the joys of a good woman.

Chapter Seven

Jax stood at the precipice and looked down. The Hollywood hills were not so aptly named—Hollywood chasms would have been more appropriate. Some of the ravines were narrow and deep, a dangerous place for those who didn't know the hazards.

He picked up the harness he'd rigged for Nicole and checked the knots one more time. His work was always dangerous, and normally he took it in stride. For some reason, though, he wanted to double-check everything involving Nicole.

Jason recoiled the ropes and put them in a neat pile. "Looks like we're ready whenever O.J. gets the camera angle he wants."

"I think he's waiting for 'the glorious colors of sunset.'" Jax wasn't mocking the cinematographer. A lot of the art of filmmaking was done at the camera lens. But often stunt safety and artistic need ran counter to each other. Jax was always more concerned for his stunt crew.

"I hope he takes into consideration the time factor. That light lasts about ten minutes at best. Nicole is going to have to scale down here, swing a number of times, hit that one target so she can pick up the jewels and then start the ascent.''

"If we don't get it just right, we'll be back here tomorrow evening," Jax conceded.

"And John Hudson will be chewing our ass all day tomorrow. The shooting schedule is off by nearly a week. That's going to affect the budget.''

Jax gave Jason a look that said "enough.''

"Okay, okay," Jason said, holding up both hands. "I know we can't change things. It's just that I'd feel a lot better if we could put Nicole over the side here while there's still good light.''

"Me, too," Jax admitted. He looked down in the gully again. "I'm going to slide down and make the swing," he said. "I want to be sure that the bag of jewels is right where she can grab it.''

"Good idea.''

Jax clamped on his harness, grabbed up several coils of rope and headed to the edge. He swung the rope over the rusted iron hulk of what once was a bridge. He'd already checked it out thoroughly to be sure it would hold both his weight and Nicole's. He was seriously considering hanging below Nicole in case she had trouble starting her swing.

As he let the rope slide through his glove-covered hands, he dropped rapidly into the gully. It was an eerie sensation. Halfway to his destination, he started a gentle swing on the rope.

The canyon was narrow and he began to calculate the arc of his swing, realizing he'd have to adjust it to a more westerly direction. He fought back an urge to cancel the entire stunt and adjusted his swing. It wasn't that difficult to do. Nicole could handle it. She was a pro when it came to stunts.

In a few moments he found himself moving closer and closer to the craggy wall of the ravine. Enough daylight prevailed to illuminate the small indention where the prop man had placed the bag of fake jewels.

They were within easy reach for Nicole. He felt the knot relaxing in his stomach.

"Jax, Nicole's here. You want me to send her on down?" Jason called out to him.

"Let me check her harness." Jax didn't want to take a single chance. He was feeling better about the stunt, but still, there was a part of him that wouldn't totally relax.

"It's okay, Jax. I have the harness on and I'm coming down. Wait for me." Nicole was calling out to him as she perched on the bridge rafter.

"Wait," he said. He wanted to check the fit of the harness on her. "Just wait!"

But it was too late. He saw her body begin to descend to him. He wanted to curse, but he held himself back. Nicole was a professional. She knew how to check her harness. She knew what she was doing. He'd have to hold on to that and let her do her work.

She came down fast, and Jax forced a smile as she drew parallel to him. "Let's get this over with," she said, smiling. He could see her grip on the rope was deathlike. Nicole, once again, was facing her fears. He gave her a smile of encouragement.

"Swing a little more westerly than we planned. There's a hunk of rock in the way. Just adjust a little and the jewels are right where we calculated would make the easiest retrieval. Grab them, hold them up for the camera to see, and then we'll pull you up, okay?"

"I've got it," Nicole said. "Angela's on the ridge, waiting to take over the show. Elvis is there, too."

"And Familiar?" Jax asked.

"I haven't seen him since he threw that brownie and ice cream on Monica." She gave a small giggle. "I would give anything to have that on tape. I think I could watch it every night before I went to bed."

"That's not very gracious, Nicole," Jax teased her. "In fact, that sounds a little vengeful."

"Perhaps," she said without a qualm. "Then I'm vengeful. Still, it was a high point of my career. Familiar is one smart cat."

"Indeed," Jax said.

"Hey, you two down there, quit gabbing and let's see some action," Jason called. "Jax, get out of the shot. O.J. wants to frame it up."

"I'm going down," Jax said. "My rope will blend into the rocks."

"Fine, just get out of the way!" Jason waved him to the side.

"I'm ready to get this done and get back up to terra firma," Nicole said. "Did you have any luck contacting Richard Weeks?"

"Some. He lives in Sherman Oaks, which doesn't surprise me. I left a message but didn't get a call back. Maybe I'll hear something when we get back."

"Great. We'll talk up top."

Nicole was a slender silhouette framed by the magnificent orange glow of the setting sun as Jax dropped lower on his rope and angled toward the cliff face where his rope would blend in with the rocks and wouldn't show up on the film.

With perfect coordination he watched her lower herself as she began to swing so that she could reach the cliff wall and pick up the sack of jewels.

She was a pleasure to watch. She didn't waste a single movement. That was one thing that made her so good at her job. She knew how to maximize every effort. It was the trick of the best stuntmen. Nicole had a great career ahead of her as a stuntwoman. But she could also step forward as a leading lady. She had the looks and the talent, if she had the desire to stay that long in the eye of the camera. He, personally, preferred the stunt work. He didn't like giving up his privacy for fame. But that was his choice. As he watched Nicole swing ever closer to the cliff face, he knew that she would soon have to choose herself. Her talents were becoming more and more appreciated.

Concern touched Jax. Nicole was a little high for the jewels, he realized, as she swung closer to the cliff. He waited for her to realize her miscalculation and adjust her rope.

Jax hung motionless, watching, as he saw her extend her hand. The next instant was a blur of action as something launched itself from the side of the cliff. The feathered creature, shrieking furiously, dove straight at Nicole.

He saw her overreact, throwing her body out of the way of the bird. As she did so, she lost her hold on her rope and began to flip backward in slow motion. The rope slipped through her hands as she hung from the harness, her body starting to slip out of the knots that should have held her.

Jax had no time to call her name or even yell instructions at her. He was already climbing toward her. The brown-feathered creature made another dive at Nicole before it circled and flew away. On the edge of his consciousness Jax registered that it was a hawk. It had undoubtedly been nesting just above the place the fake jewels had been left.

He was right below Nicole, and he narrowed his focus on her. He felt something wet drop onto his face. When he wiped it with his hand and looked at it, he was horrified to discover that it was blood.

Nicole was dangling two hundred feet above a ravine and she was bleeding.

"Don't panic, Nicole," he whispered up to her. "I'm right beneath you. Another fifty yards and I'll be there." She was held precariously by her hips. The harness had been designed to hold her in a sitting position. Now, with the shift in her weight, Nicole might slip out!

"Stay down," she said in a voice surprisingly strong. "I'm okay. The bird attacked me and I lost the rope, but I'm okay now. I just have to pull myself back upright.''

And she began to lever her upper torso back upright as she spoke. "Stay out of the shot, Jax. I don't want to do this again. I'm okay.''

Jax held back, his heart pounding so loudly he wondered that the camera crew didn't yell out to him to be quiet.

There wasn't a sound from the camera crew or the supporting cast on the bridge, and Jax knew that O. J. Adams had given everyone strict orders to remain totally silent. Nicole had unintentionally given him some dramatic footage that would only add to the scene—if she survived.

Nicole began to slowly start her swing toward the cliff face again. This time she dropped down another fifteen feet. She was right on target. Jax held his breath as she swung closer and closer to the jewels. The sun was setting, the light going from brilliant orange to a rosy red. Nicole was going to have to hurry and complete this in one shot or none of it would be usable. It would be impossible to duplicate the magnificence of the current sunset on another day.

She seemed to realize that, too, as she swung hard and reached out with her hand.

Her triumphant yell could be heard echoing through the ravine as she held the sack of fake jewels aloft and shook them for added emphasis.

Following the script, a series of gunshots echoed through the ravine. Nicole ducked, making her body as small a target as possible, and began the ascent. The wall of the ravine beside her burst and splintered with the small detonators the prop crew had inserted in the stone. Nicole kept climbing.

Jax couldn't see what the cameraman was doing, but he knew that now the shot would swing up to the bridge where Angela was dressed identically to Nicole. She, too, held a bag of jewels. Her shout of triumph echoed Nicole's. And it was done.

The sound of John Hudson's voice came over a megaphone. "That's a wrap, folks. Get Nicole up and make sure she isn't hurt. What the hell was that thing?"

Jax felt his own ropes being pulled and he knew that Jason and the other crewmembers were hard at work. As his feet touched the bridge and he grasped the rail, he didn't think he'd ever been happier to get back on firm ground.

Nicole was right beside him and she gave him a big grin and a thumbs-up sign.

"No one warned me about the bird," she said.

"No one knew about the bird," Jax pointed out. "But they should have. I thought the prop men were all over this cliff day before yesterday." He looked at Jason who shrugged.

Jax didn't have time to ask any more questions. John Hudson was on the bridge. His concern was for Nicole, who had a gash on her forearm where the bird's talon had ripped through her cat suit and her skin.

"Nasty, nasty looking," John said. "Does anyone know what kind of bird it was?"

"My best guess would be a hawk," Jax said. He wasn't an authority on birds of prey, but the fury and swiftness of the attack reminded him of things he'd read about hawks. They were highly territorial, and they defended their nests with everything they had.

"Did you see a nest?" he asked Nicole.

"I truly didn't have time to see anything. The light wasn't the best. I just knew I was up too high for the jewels, but I was going to push off the cliff face and drop down. My mistake."

Jax wanted to put his arms around her and hug her, to make sure she was really there, safe and only with minor injuries. But he didn't. Nicole was being led away by a medic to get her arm tended to, and Jax was left with John.

"That's some of the best footage I've ever seen," John said. "O.J. said he had her perfect. This will add even more drama to the story. And that bird! We have the most remarkable trained cat, but that bird deserves at least a credit line in the movie."

Jax nodded. He was waiting for a moment alone with John. All around him the crew was gathering the ropes and other props, loading the cameras up, and preparing to call it quits for the night. Darkness was falling rapidly, and several of the huge camera lights had been turned on to make it easier for the workmen.

John stood in the midst of it all, going over the next day's shooting schedule. When Nicole returned, he put his arm around her. "That was magnificent, Nicole. You showed your mettle then. Any other person would have screamed or given up. But you made it work, and it will be magnificent. I also owe you for bringing Ms. King to the set. That girl has more natural talent in her little finger than most actresses I've worked with. How about I take you to dinner tomorrow night?"

Jax felt his jaw begin to drop before he stopped it. John Hudson wasn't known for putting moves on young actresses. He was a serious filmmaker.

"I'm sorry, but I already have plans," Nicole said smoothly. "How about lunch instead?"

"That would be fine. There's something I want to talk to you about. In private."

"Lunch, then," Nicole said, sounding a little more nervous than she had before.

"And again, thanks. You are marvelous." John brushed a kiss on her cheek and turned away.

"I'll be right back," Jax said as he followed John. He caught him a few yards away. Glancing around, Jax realized that he had about as much privacy as he could expect.

"Mr. Hudson," he said, "you're aware that Nicole is having some legal difficulties."

"Yes, I am." John's tone was frosty.

"I'm helping Nicole. She's a friend of mine. And I just have to ask you something."

"Ask away. That doesn't mean I'll answer."

Jax continued, though he knew the director was

getting aggravated with him. "I saw Monica Kane on the set today. I heard she was replacing Kim Lumet."

"That's true."

"How well do you know Ms. Kane?"

"That isn't any of your business. In fact, I can't see where any of this is your business."

"Ms. Kane made it a point of trying to humiliate Nicole in the canteen today. She brought up Nicole's father and the Dream of Isis. Let's just say that subtlety isn't Ms. Kane's strong suit. My question, sir, is do you know Monica Kane well enough to know if she told the truth the night the Dream of Isis was stolen?"

"That's not a question for me to answer. And young man, I advise you to stay out of the past. Time doesn't heal all wounds, and the Dream of Isis is one issue that won't go away. I'm sorry for Nicole, but I can't help you."

John walked away without a backward glance.

When Jax rejoined Nicole, she was letting one of the costume women cut the sleeve out of her cat suit. It had been shredded.

"I guess I'm going to be tough on the costume budget," she said, smiling. She held up the bag of jewels she'd retrieved from the ravine. "I forgot to give these to the prop men."

"No harm done," Jax said. He was still baffled by John Hudson's reaction. "Let's get out of here."

"Sounds good to me."

They were about to leave when Angela Myers

stepped out of the shadows. "Nicole!" she called out, throwing something at Nicole's chest.

Nicole caught the second bag of fake jewels against her chest, holding them with her good arm.

"Give these to the prop men," Angela said, her tone an order.

"Angela, what are you still doing here?" Jax asked in a still voice. "I thought you left a while ago."

"Oh, I had to see what additional little moment of drama Nicole might try to stir up."

"Maybe I should put you in the harness and lower you into the ravine," Nicole said. "That would do my heart good."

"Empty threats," Angela said. "Just be sure the prop man gets his gear back. They're only fakes, though, so you won't be tempted to steal them."

She sauntered off the bridge.

"I'd like to show her what she can do with these fake jewels," Nicole said angrily.

Jax put his arm around her. "Angela is up to something. I just haven't figured what it is."

JAX AND NICOLE have been at the bridge shoot for nearly an hour now. I haven't got a lot of time left to figure out O.J.'s computer. It's one of the most sophisticated things I've ever run across. But I'm about to get it. There, I have Internet access now, and I'm off to do a serious search.

First, I want to explore Monica Kane. I wasn't born when she was up for her Oscar. She's a lovely woman on the exterior, but there's some real rot inside. Bitter, bitter. But why?

Let's see, Oscars in 1983. Here's the list of nominees, and I see she didn't win. There are stories from the Hollywood Reporter *and other industry rags. Hummm. Not even a hint of sympathy for Monica, but there is one interesting slant to this story that says the loss of the stone could turn events around and swing the Academy into giving Monica the Oscar out of pity. But no, Monica lost out.*

And what is this! A sidebar story about her romance with…John Hudson! Wow! Now, that's some gossip that might have meaning.

She and John were a big item. He was planning on shooting her next film. And they were setting a wedding date. But they never married. Or maybe they did. Let me read on. Let's see, here the story picks up with their breakup, which came shortly after the Oscars.

And here's a photo of Monica with her new man. None other than Richard Weeks, wealthy Hollywood real-estate mogul.

My, oh, my. Let me hit the print button on all of this. I want to be sure to take a copy to Nicole and Jax.

Now I'll dig a little deeper and see if there's a story about Vincent Paul. Sure enough, it's all being hashed and rehashed as part of the Oscar night hullabaloo. Here's the story on Vincent, who proclaimed his innocence as he was led away from his store in handcuffs. And look! In the window is little

Nicole looking out and crying. It's a Pulitzer photo, but one that breaks my heart.

The story says the diamond was taken from the store between midnight and six in the morning. Vincent closed shop late, went home with his daughter, then returned to find the diamond missing. He was charged in under four hours. The diamond was never found.

I'll print this, too, but I'll only show this to Jax. I don't want to remind Nicole of all the things she's lost. Well, it's time to make my getaway. I don't want O.J. to catch me here. He seems cat friendly, but you never know what dark impulses lurk beneath the facade of a humanoid.

Chapter Eight

Now that the adrenaline rush was over, Nicole felt as if the marrow had been sucked from her bones. Her muscles were Jell-O, and she wanted a nice vodka martini and a hot bath. And that was exactly what she intended to have as soon as she got home.

To her disgust, she found that the prop men had already packed up and gone. She was left with both bags of fake jewels, which meant she'd have to be up on the set early to turn them in. They might be needed in the first scenes for the next day's shooting.

It was just like Angela to leave her holding the bag—literally.

"You look mighty serious," Jax said as he opened the door of his truck. He'd offered to drive her home.

"That Angela." She held up the bags. "I have to turn them in to property tomorrow first thing."

"I'll do it," Jax said. "I have to get up anyway."

"Are you sure?" Nicole wasn't a late sleeper, but this was one time she needed the luxury of sleeping until she awoke naturally.

"Positive. I have to be on the set at seven to check

out a scene with Familiar. He has to walk that window ledge tomorrow and I want to be sure everything is tip-top perfect.''

''Yes, we want to take care of Familiar,'' Nicole said.

She leaned back against the seat as Jax drove. In the truck he was a far more conservative driver. Still, the motorcycle ride had been exhilarating. She smiled as she thought about it.

''Nicole, was there anyone who would benefit from the destruction of your father's reputation?''

Nicole opened her eyes, suddenly wide-awake. All fatigue fled. ''The jewelry design business is terribly competitive. When Dad got almost all of the business for the Oscar nominees, there was a lot of grumbling and anger among the other design houses. They felt Dad had an inside track. The truth was that he went to the trouble of seeing the films, watching the stars, checking with the design houses that were making their dresses and then creating a jewelry design that complemented all of the elements. He had sort of a whole-universe approach to the project and it paid off.''

''Were some of these competitors so angered that they would steal the Dream of Isis just to ruin your father?''

Nicole took a long, deep breath. ''I don't know. I can't really answer that. I was only a kid. I remember arguments and bitter accusations from a couple of designers. Chadwick Elliot for one. He was horrible.

But would he deliberately ruin my father?'' She shook her head. ''I can't say.''

''Did Mr. Elliot pick up your father's business?''

''Almost all of it,'' Nicole said. She really hadn't framed her father's conviction in terms of someone else's monetary gain, but now that Jax was forcing her to do it, she had begun to see Chadwick Elliot in another light.

''Could he have staged the burglary?''

''He knew the shop. He came by on a regular basis. Sort of that friendly rival type of relationship, until Dad got the Oscar commissions. Chadwick frequently talked with Dad about security measures.'' She paused for a few seconds. ''In fact, I'm remembering that just before the burglary, he talked to Dad extensively about the type of security he had in the store. Chadwick wanted to upgrade his system, he said.''

''Did your father tell this to the police?''

''I don't know,'' Nicole said. ''Probably not. I honestly don't think it would cross Dad's mind that one of his competitors would deliberately destroy him.''

''We need to have a look at that old case file. I wonder exactly how we can manage that.''

''Can we just ask?''

''That's probably a logical place to start, but if we're refused, then what? I don't believe the police have to give files to any Tom, Dick or Harry who asks for them.''

''Then you can pretend to be a private investigator,'' Nicole said, excitement in her voice. ''The prop department has plenty of badges and license cards. We can find something that works, I'm sure.''

She could see Jax wasn't head over heels in love with the plan, but it beat the alternative—breaking in to the police department.

''I'm not an actor,'' Jax pointed out.

''But you could be.'' Nicole wasn't going to take no for an answer. It was the easiest way to get to see the file.

''I'll think about it.'' Jax parked in front of her trailer. The lights were on inside and Connie opened the door wide, a smile of welcome on her face.

''I've made some chicken enchiladas for dinner,'' Connie said, her T-shirt bearing witness to her culinary labors. ''And some guy named Carlos Sanchez has been calling for you, Nicole. He said he needed to talk with you as soon as you got in.''

''Will you stay for dinner?'' Nicole asked Jax. ''It would hurt Connie's feelings if you didn't.''

''Sure. I've never met an enchilada I didn't like.''

Nicole left Jax in the kitchen sipping a Corona while Connie drank a cola. Nicole used the phone in her bedroom to talk to the lawyer. Her father had probably called Sanchez and gigged him into action. Well, she was just going to fire him. They didn't have the money he expected from his clients.

''Ms. Paul,'' Sanchez said in his very refined voice. ''We need to talk.''

''I'm sorry, Mr. Sanchez. My father was out of

line when he hired you. We simply can't afford your services.''

''Oh, but you misunderstand. I'm taking the case pro bono. After your father's wrongful conviction, I feel I owe you something.''

Nicole was so astounded she had to sit down on the bed. Carlos Sanchez wasn't a Good Samaritan. He didn't take cases for free. Not ever. And he didn't have a conscience, so his couldn't be hurting about her father.

''What did you want to talk to me about?'' She decided to change the focus while she tried to sort through this unexpected turn of events.

''I'm worried about your father.''

The words were like little darts of lightning into her heart. ''Why? What happened?''

''Vincent is obsessed with the idea that your current troubles stem from the theft of the Dream of Isis. He's called me four times today to tell me things he's just remembered.''

''And?''

''Well, it is a little intrusive, but more than that, I don't think it's good for his health.''

''And you want me to speak to him?''

''That would be helpful. He's threatening to call the police and have the case reopened. From my point of view, all of this will only complicate your case. Vincent is stirring the hornet's nest and I fear it is you who will get stung.''

''Of course I'll talk to him. Once I explain it that way, I'm sure he'll back off.'' Nicole wasn't certain of that at all, but she intended to stress to her father that he wasn't helping. What Carlos Sanchez said made sense. The police weren't interested in a case they solved twenty years prior. Vincent's phone calls would only prove irritating.

"Thank you, Nicole. I'll be in touch when we have your arraignment set. It shouldn't be long."

"I also have a favor," Nicole said. "I'd like to see your file on my father's case."

There was a long pause. "Surely you don't subscribe to your father's ridiculous belief that the two cases are connected!"

"If I had the file, I might be able to show him they aren't," Nicole countered. "You do have the file, correct?"

"I can't be certain. That was a long time ago. But you're welcome to stop by the office and I'll have an assistant look for it."

"That would be wonderful," Nicole said, making her voice sound full of respect. "I'll be by tomorrow after lunch."

"And you'll speak to your father?"

"Tonight," she promised. "Dad loves me and he's trying to help me. But I'll convince him that he's only making matters worse."

"Good evening, Nicole."

The line was dead and Nicole replaced the phone. She sat staring at it for a moment. Carlos Sanchez was a man with a battery of secretaries. If he didn't want to take a call there was no way in hell to get through to him. Yet he was acting like he couldn't deflect the nuisance calls of an old man. Why? It was just another little mystery to add to the stack that had begun to creep from her ankles up her thighs.

JAX INSISTED on helping wash the dishes, and when he was finished, he decided it was time to head home. Nicole looked completely done in. The call from Carlos Sanchez and the subsequent conversation with her father—where she'd tried to convince him not to call the lawyer and certainly not to annoy the police—had worn her out. Jax, too, felt tired. He was about to say his good-nights when he heard the sound of scratching at the door.

Connie opened the door and a black shadow with a piece of white paper darted inside.

"What in the world?" Connie said, catching the cat and taking the paper from his mouth. "What's this?" She handed it to Jax.

It took only a moment for Jax to find the pertinent information on the sheet. John Hudson and Monica Kane. They had, for a brief moment, been *the* Hollywood couple. And he also had his explanation about John's brusque behavior at the bridge.

Jax handed the sheet to Nicole, who read it and passed it to Connie.

"I find that hard to believe. Why would John involve himself with that she-cat?" Connie asked. "I met her today for the first time. I had some paper and a pen for her autograph. She almost spit on me."

Jax saw Nicole grinning and he couldn't suppress his own smile of amusement. "Don't be too naive,

Connie. Monica is a very beautiful woman. Twenty years ago I'm sure she was irresistible. And she can be charming, when it suits her purposes.''

''And mean as a scorpion. On the set today she treated me like I had leprosy. When she found out that I was from Arkansas, she acted like it was contagious. She was awful.''

''She is awful, but she's also awfully beautiful,'' Nicole pointed out.

''Looks don't last near long enough,'' Connie said. ''My mama always told me that being pretty didn't give a girl license to hurt others.''

''Your mother is right, but obviously Monica missed that lesson,'' Nicole said. She looked at Jax. He'd already told her about John's strange behavior when he'd asked him about Monica and the diamond.

''This whole thing gets more and more tangled,'' Jax said speculatively. ''But all threads lead back to that damn diamond. Your father may well be on to something.''

''I can't wait to see that case file tomorrow,'' Nicole said. ''I'm glad I remembered that Sanchez would probably have a copy, though I was looking forward to seeing you act like a tough P.I.''

''Me-ow!'' Familiar said.

Nicole laughed. ''I guess one tough P.I. is enough on any case, and we have Familiar to thank for this lead.''

''And for helping me,'' Connie said. ''I just wonder what he's going to do next?''

''We'll find out tomorrow,'' Jax said. ''And on

that note, I'd better go.'' He looked longingly at Nicole. What he really wanted was to stay—in her bed. Fragments of his erotic dream kept popping into his head. Nicole had invaded his fantasy life and was creeping more and more into his daylight thoughts. In fact, he hardly thought about anything except her now. And he hadn't even kissed her.

''I'll walk you out,'' she said, as if she'd read his mind.

''I have to study my scene,'' Connie said. ''I'll be way back in my room, with the door shut, and the radio on, and I won't come out for at least three hours.'' She grinned like an imp as she left them alone.

''Not very subtle, is she?'' Jax asked.

''Maybe we weren't, either.''

Jax felt that sweet tightening in his stomach, the first flutter of desire. He didn't wait for an invitation. He slipped his arms around Nicole and kissed her.

Her arms went around his neck and she clung to him, kissing him back without reserve. They went from start to full-blown passion in less than sixty seconds. Jax knew that if he didn't break off the kiss, he was going to have to sleep with her.

''Nicole,'' he whispered, ''are you sure?''

She slowly stiffened in his arms and he had his answer.

''You shouldn't have asked that question,'' she said, her voice rough with emotion. ''I was sure. Until you asked. And then it brought back every time I've counted on someone in the past. Just about the time I really believed they were there for me, they left.'' She leaned her forehead against his chest. ''I'm terrified you'll do the same. I'm afraid if I really allow myself to feel all of this for you, then you'll leave.''

Jax forced his own passion to calm. Now he needed reason, not throbbing libido. This was more important than satisfying his own desires. ''It's okay,'' he said gently. ''Really it is. I think we both want to make sure we don't rush into this.''

''But I want to rush into it,'' Nicole said. She looked up and her gaze held anguish and despair. ''I don't want to live like this. I really want to be a girl who can just take joy in the moment and not keep expecting the other shoe to fall.''

Jax smiled, and then he teased the corners of her mouth gently with his thumb until she smiled. ''If only it were that easy,'' he said, ''but the bottom line is that trust has to be addressed sometime in each relationship. We're just going to do it at the beginning rather than in the middle, okay?''

He saw the tension ease around her eyes. ''Jax, where did you come from? How was I lucky enough to find you in my life?''

''Those questions are a whole lot easier to answer than the ones we're facing regarding your father and the Dream of Isis.''

''I'm not so sure,'' Nicole said.

''I am.'' He pulled her into his arms and held her, kissing the top of her head and gently lifting her chin for a tender, gentle kiss. Even though he was deliberately holding himself back, just the feel of her soft lips was enough to nearly break his firm resolve to take things slowly with Nicole.

He eased back from her. "We have a lot of future ahead of us, Nicole. We have plenty of time."

"Who are you trying to convince?" she asked with a sad grin. "You or me?"

"Both of us," he said. "Both of us. Now I really had better go."

He stepped to the door and opened it. Familiar shot out of the trailer before he could stop him. "Where the heck is that cat going to?" he asked.

"Your truck," Nicole said. "Look. He's hopping in the window."

"He's got one of those jewelry bags I'm taking to the prop department," Jax said. "He's bringing it up here."

"I wonder what he's up to." Nicole took the bag that Familiar brought to her. "What shall I do with it?"

She had her answer when Familiar jumped up and pulled it from her hands. In a flash he was working the knot that held it together.

"Let me help," Jax said. He untied the knot and slowly dumped the contents of the sack on the trailer floor.

The jewels were fake, but they were quality fakes. Jax sorted through them, holding each one up for the cat to inspect.

"Look at the sapphire broach!" Nicole said with excitement. "It isn't a fake."

"What?" Jax picked up the piece she indicated. "How can you tell?"

"I'm the daughter of a jeweler. Trust me, those are real sapphires, and that is a very valuable piece."

"So what's it doing in the bag of fake jewels?" Jax asked. He knew the answer instantly.

"Damn that Angela. She was trying to deliberately set you up again." Jax stood up, furious. "And we almost walked right into her trap."

"Except that in the morning, when the cops come again, you would have had possession of the jewel," Nicole pointed out. "What are we going to do?" Nicole asked as she stroked Familiar. "Thank goodness for the cat!"

"He is something else," Jax said, scratching Familiar under the chin while the cat purred. "As to what we're going to do, we're going to turn the tables."

"How?"

"I want you to call Angela. Tell her something, anything, to get her out of her trailer. Then I'm going to plant this bag of jewels on her, just like she tried to do to you."

Nicole's smile told of her approval of the plan. "Perfect, Jax. That's perfect. Now, what would draw Angela out of her trailer long enough to accomplish this?"

"I'm not sure," Jax said.

Nicole's smile widened into a grin. "I am. You call her and tell her that you have to see her. Tell her that you're attracted to her and can no longer hide what you feel.''

"I can't do that!" Jax protested. "That would be the worst lie I've ever told.''

"But it would hook her. She'd have to see you, even if it was to crush you. Angela's biggest weak point is her vanity and this would play right into her hands.''

Jax considered it. "You're right, I suppose, but if this gets all over the set, I'll be ruined.''

"Trust me, once you lower the boom on her, she won't tell this to anyone.''

"But then you'll have to break in to her trailer and hide the jewels.''

"You forget, I'm a fairly competent stuntwoman. I think I can manage a flimsy trailer. Besides, it won't take but a few seconds to stuff the sack behind the pillows on her sofa. She won't be expecting this, so she won't be looking for anything.''

Jax nodded. "I don't like it, but I think it'll work.''

"Good.'' Nicole handed him the phone. "I can't wait to hear what you have to say to Angela.''

"Meow!'' Familiar hopped to the sofa. One black paw patted the second bag of jewels. "Meow!'' he demanded.

Jax hesitated with the phone in his hand. "The cat's trying to tell us something,'' he said.

"What?'' Nicole knelt down by Familiar. "Is there something about this bag?'' she picked it up.

"Of course there's something about that bag,'' Jax said. "How do we know which of the bags Angela gave you? The sapphire broach could have been in the bag you retrieved from the ravine.''

"You're right,'' Nicole said, exhaling. ''Thank goodness for Familiar. I'd already tried and convicted Angela of setting me up. I was making the same mistake everyone made about Dad.''

Jax put his hand on her shoulder. "Not quite,'' he said, ''and I was right at your side. Angela was the logical choice.'' He held out the portable phone. ''So should I call her?''

Nicole shook her head. "I don't know what to do.''

Familiar picked up the bag of jewels with the broach inside. He trotted to the door. "Meow,'' he said, scratching with one paw.

"He obviously has outthought us, and he has a plan,'' Jax said with a degree of dry humor.

"He is, after all, an extraordinarily smart cat,'' Nicole conceded.

"Let's see what he's up to.''

Chapter Nine

My gut instinct tells me that Nicole and Jax were right on target when they named Angela as the culprit who tried to stick them with a valuable broach, but my training as a P.I. tells me not to jump to conclusions. We don't have enough evidence to pin this on Angela outright.

And the truth is, almost everyone has access to the props. Anyone could have put that sapphire broach in the bag, and it would be a pretty easy guess that Nicole might end up with the bag in her possession.

So my plan is one of cunning. I'm going to stash this little sack of jewels under Angela's trailer. It will point the finger of suspicion at her, but it will be in a place where anyone could have left it. All in all, I think it's the best plan until we figure out who really is behind the sapphire broach.

Nicole and Jax are hiding behind some vehicles watching. Now I'll just slip under here, stash the bag above this pipe and we're home free. Tomorrow I think I'll enlist Elvis to help me "find" the bag at just the proper moment.

This is going to be rich. Now, if only I could implicate Monica Kane in this. I'm telling you, Monica and Angela are cut from the same evil cloth. A little lesson in humility would be good for both of them.

The inspired part of this plan is that if Angela suggests that Nicole might have the sapphire broach when it's found under Angela's trailer, it will go a long way toward coloring the first jewelry theft as a setup, too. I must say, sometimes my ideas border on pure genius.

I'm glad my hunch paid off about the bag of jewels. Every kitty instinct I had urged me to check out the contents of the bags. It just seemed too convenient to me that Nicole would be left with two leather bags of jewels—even fake ones—after she'd been accused of stealing jewelry. Even though the jewels are costume, some of them are expensive. It just didn't sit right.

I have a big problem here with Nicole and Jax. They're far too trusting. I'm going to have to give them a crash course in sniffing out ulterior motives. And I can see that's got to happen sooner rather than later. With humanoids, the learning curve is a little ungraded, so I'll have to figure out a quick method of clueing them in.

After my venture onto the Internet earlier this evening, I spent some time picking up facts the old-fashioned way—eavesdropping.

Wandering around the set, I was privy to a lot of interesting commentary.

No one on the set seems to realize that cats can

comprehend everything humans say. Simply because we don't talk back or respond, people assume we're not capable of understanding. That's biped reasoning for you. Of course it would never occur to a humanoid to keep silent by choice. They are far more like apes than even they know. Chatter, chatter, chatter.

But I can comprehend everything that's said around me. As can all cats, dogs, horses, wolves— the list is endless. So why don't we respond?

Think of it this way. What's the first thing that would happen to me if I let on that I spoke fluent English? I can tell you. I'd have to get a job. I'd be expected to become a worker bee, like the humanoids. As it stands now, I have the best of both worlds. I get everything I want, and I work when I choose.

I heard the moron Kyle Lancer referring to me as a dumb animal. At least I'm not on the telephone every half hour making appointments for hair transplants, chin implants and the like.

It's not that I'm not vain. I am. But I'm also naturally handsome and refined. And in order to maintain my incredible good looks, I think it's time to saunter on home for a little shut-eye. I have an early call in the morning with Jax, and I certainly want to be on hand when the alarm is sounded about the jewels. This is going to be fun!

JAX HAD JUST finished the scene with Familiar when he saw the cat's ears prick forward. A few seconds later he, too, saw the patrol cars pull into the lot. So, it had begun. Now he'd be able to learn a few very important facts that would point the finger at the person who was trying to sabotage Nicole's career.

"Let's go," he said to Familiar. Together they hurried to join the crowd gathering around John Hudson.

"We have a report of a stolen broach," Officer Steve Greene said. "We got a call from one of your cast, Monica Kane. She said someone had taken a sapphire broach of great value."

"A stolen broach?" John was surprised. "Monica is saying someone stole her broach? I haven't heard a word about it."

"That's correct, sir," the officer said. "Could you tell us where we might locate Ms. Kane?"

"Her trailer is right over there."

"I'll be glad to show the officers," Jax said. More than glad, he thought to himself. This was one scene he didn't want to miss.

"Thank you, Jax," John said. "If that's agreeable with the officers. I'm on a tight shooting schedule, and we need to keep working. Oh, Jax, could you please tell Nicole we'll have to cancel lunch today? I'll get with her and set another time. There's something we really must discuss, but I can't manage it today." He turned back to direct the cinematographer on the next shots.

Jax walked the two lawmen to the door of Monica's trailer, Familiar at his heels. Both of them stepped back as Officer Greene knocked.

"I'm so glad you've arrived," Monica said, opening the door wide and almost flinging herself on the lawmen. "I can't believe this has happened to me again. You realize I was the victim of a terrible theft some twenty years ago when I was nominated for an Oscar."

To Jax's total amusement, the policemen were unmoved by Monica's theatrics or her constant references to her past glories.

Working very efficiently, the officers took the report and then examined Monica's trailer. They immediately found marks that indicated the door had been jimmied open. Monica, of course, denied noticing them. Jax took it all in while Familiar flicked his tail in irritation.

"Whoever is behind this is doing a really good job of setting Nicole up," Jax whispered to the cat.

"Meow," Familiar agreed in a soft tone.

"Has anyone told you officers that there's a woman working here with a criminal record for jewelry theft?" Monica asked.

"Who would that be?" Officer Greene asked.

"Nicole Paul. Her trailer is right over there. She's living with another jailbird. Some hillbilly kid from Arkansas who thinks just because she's eighteen she'll look good on the silver screen."

The officer got on his shoulder mike and in a moment he was speaking softly with his partner.

"Thanks for the help, ma'am. We'll send some forensic technicians to take fingerprints around the door and from the case where the broach was taken.

Odd that nothing else was taken. You have an impressive assortment of jewelry.''

"It was the most valuable piece I had with me," Monica said. "Just like that last time. The only jewel stolen then was the Dream of Isis. Once that stone was taken, my life was ruined. I didn't win the Oscar and I was forever more associated with that blasted curse. It's ruined my dreams. Everyone instantly assumes that I'm tainted."

Jax and the cat stared at each other. "The curse," Jax said. He'd failed to find out exactly what the curse of the Dream of Isis was. Most likely something to do with bad luck, but it would be interesting to know the actual mojo the stone allegedly carried.

"We'll be in touch," the officers said as they escaped from Monica's accusations and demands.

Jax took a different route to Nicole's trailer, but he arrived just as the officers did. Nicole invited them in, signaling Jax and Familiar inside also.

"Connie, would you make a pot of coffee for us?" Nicole asked.

"Sure." Connie gave the policemen a critical look. "But I'm just in the kitchen if you need me."

Jax found the comment endearing. Connie had become a loyal supporter of Nicole.

"Ms. Kane has reported her broach missing," Officer Greene stated.

"Oh, really," Nicole said. "How unfortunate. What type of broach was it?"

The officer explained about the missing jewelry and deftly moved into his questions. Nicole answered all of them, telling the officers that the only jewelry she had was a bag of cosmetic jewelry for the movie. Having said all that, she retrieved the second bag and handed it to the officers.

After examining the bag, they returned it to her. "There's nothing like the broach Ms. Kane described here," Officer Greene said. "Would you mind if we looked around?"

"Am I a suspect?" Nicole asked.

"No, ma'am. Not exactly a suspect, but you have been charged with theft in another incident."

"That's the silliest thing I ever heard." Connie had brought the coffee into the small den on a tray. She set it down and put her hands on her hips. "Nicole is one of the best people on this earth. I can't believe anyone would even hint that she might steal something. I'll bet Monica put her stupid broach somewhere and forgot where she put it. That's like her to start a stink and blame everyone else."

"It's okay, Connie. I don't mind if the officers search the trailer. I don't have a thing to hide. Just finish your coffee and look wherever you'd like," Nicole said easily.

The policemen made short work of their coffee and their search. When they were finished, Officer Greene thanked Nicole for her cooperation.

"No problem," she said. "You know, the prop department has additional jewels. I wonder if Ms. Kane's broach could have mistakenly gotten mixed in with those. I mean this is a movie about a jewel thief. It wouldn't be impossible for Monica to have removed her broach during a costume change and somehow it got picked up and put among the other costume jewels.'' As she talked Nicole led the officers to the door and out into the April sunshine.

Officer Greene nodded. ''We'll check into that for sure.''

''And I had only one of the bags of costume jewels yesterday. I believe Angela Myers had the other. You might want to check with her.''

The anguished cry of a cat tore across the lot. The officers and everyone else immediately turned toward the sound, which was coming from beneath Angela's trailer.

Two black cats tumbled out into the dust. They separated and then tore into each other again. Clumps of fur flew into the air and the sound of total, unrestrained fury came from the cats' throats.

''It's the star and the stunt double,'' Jax said, running toward the fighting cats. ''Officers, I may need your help. Elvis can't be injured, and we need Familiar in good shape for a scene this afternoon.''

All three men went running to break up the catfight while Nicole held Connie back.

''Aren't you going to help?'' Connie demanded, surprised at Nicole's lack of action.

''Just watch,'' Nicole whispered. ''It's Familiar's starring role. I see he convinced Elvis to help him out. I think you're going to like the outcome of this scene.''

Just as the officers arrived, Elvis darted under the trailer. When he came back out, Familiar had fled and Elvis had the jewelry sack dangling from his mouth.

''Hey, that looks like the sack of jewels Nicole was talking about,'' Jax said, taking it from the cat. Instead of opening it, he handed it over to the officers. ''Maybe you should check it for the broach.''

Officer Greene opened the sack. In a few seconds he'd picked out the broach in the jumble of jewels. He held it up. ''Well, I think the mystery of the missing broach is solved, but now there's something else to investigate. How did those jewels get under Angela Myers's trailer?''

''Now, that's a good question,'' Jax said, unable to hide his grin. ''I'll be real interested in hearing Angela's explanation.''

''I'm afraid we're going to have to talk to Angela Myers,'' Officer Greene said.

''This is the worst duty I've had in a long time,'' the other officer joked. ''I never in a million years thought I'd get to interview a movie star. If you don't want to do it, Steve, I'll be glad to question Ms. Myers by myself.''

''I think I'd better sit in on the session,'' Steve said.

Both officers were grinning when they knocked on the door of Angela's trailer.

''Whoever the hell it is, this had better be good,'' Angela was yelling as she opened the door. She stopped short when she saw the policemen.

''What?'' she asked. ''I forgot to leave a donation to the policeman's ball?''

"May we come in?" Officer Greene asked.

"No, you may not," she huffed. "I'm trying to get some rest. I have a scene this afternoon. Those darn cats fighting right under my trailer is bad enough. I can't have people knocking on my door and waking me up."

"Ma'am, we have some questions we need to ask. You can answer them here or ride down to the station with us." Officer Greene had lost his sense of humor about the situation and his voice was calm and cold.

Angela looked out at the crowd that was beginning to gather. Her gaze caught Jax's and held. The glare she shot him was red-hot with anger.

"Well, you can't stand out here making a spectacle of yourselves. Come in." She waved the officers into her trailer and then slammed the door as hard as she could.

"Mission accomplished!" Jax said as he picked Familiar up and headed for Nicole and Connie. "This cat does some awesome work."

NICOLE SAT ACROSS the vast expanse of Carlos Sanchez's desk and watched as the lawyer signed his name to a sheaf of documents while his secretary stood at his elbow, waiting.

When he was at last finished, he handed the stack of papers to Ellen and flexed his right hand to relieve the cramp.

"Thank God for Ellen," he said. "I just sign where she tells me. My whole office would fall apart if she left."

Ellen didn't even look over her shoulder as she left the office, closing the door behind her.

"Nicole, I want to be square with you. I've spoken with the officers who investigated the theft of the earring, and they feel certain you're guilty."

The harshness of the statement caught Nicole completely off guard. Of all the things she had expected, an accusation of guilt from her own attorney wasn't one of them.

"I don't care what the officers are certain of, I didn't take that earring." She rose from her chair. "I think it would be in my best interest to find a lawyer who believes in me."

"Just a minute," Carlos said, waving her back into her seat. "I didn't say *I* believed you were guilty. I merely said the officers do. Therefore they aren't willing to negotiate. They're going to play hardball on this one. I was hoping I might be able to talk them into a reduced charge, but it won't work."

"Good, because I wouldn't have pleaded guilty to a lesser charge anyway. I didn't do anything wrong. I'm not going to say I did."

Carlos shook his head. "Twenty years might have passed, but I'm reliving my first talk with your father. You sound just like him. Both of you are stubborn to a fault."

"Both of us are innocent."

Carlos looked long and hard at her. "And you see what that cost your father. I begged him to plead down if we could get a deal. He wouldn't consider it, and he served the maximum amount of time."

Nicole had no answer to that. "When will my arraignment be?"

"The courts are jammed. The backlog is indecent. I tried to get an early date, but it'll be mid-May before we can manage it. I tried to move it up, but that's the soonest we could work it out."

"That's fine. I should be through shooting this movie by then and at least it won't impact the film schedule."

"Nicole, did you talk to your father?"

She had a flash of guilt. "I'm headed there now," she said. "I had a little trouble last night and this morning." She recounted the story of the broach.

"But what would Angela Myers gain by framing you for a second theft?" Carlos asked, his face puzzled.

"Good question. I don't have an answer to what she'd gain by framing me for the first theft. At least I don't have an answer yet. But I will get one. This latest incident may help me when we go to trial, don't you think? It proves that someone is framing me for theft."

"Slim possibility." Carlos brushed it aside. "Nicole, I'm going to do my darndest to see this case never comes to trial. I know you think you want vindication, but you don't. Not in a courtroom. The cost is always too high, even when you win."

"Then I want the charges against me dropped completely."

"That would be the optimum outcome, and that's

what I'm shooting for, but I want you to be realistic.''

Nicole composed herself. She hadn't expected she'd have to fight her own lawyer. ''Did you remember to pull my father's file?'' she asked.

''Oh, yes, Ellen did that. I'm not sure how much of it is there. It's an old file and parts of it may be gone.''

''Gone?'' Nicole frowned. ''Gone where?''

''Nicole, this isn't an archive. Sometimes we pull out old cases for reference. A lot of times things don't get put back as they should.''

''How will I know what's missing?''

''If you don't miss it, then you don't need it,'' he said matter-of-factly. ''Now, I have another appointment. This is all the time I can give you. Just make sure you talk with your father, Nicole. It's more important than you know.''

''Right,'' she said, ''I'm headed there now.'' She'd find out from Vincent what he'd been doing to worry Carlos so completely.

Chapter Ten

Jax answered his cell phone on the first ring. He'd expected to hear from Nicole, but he wasn't prepared for the surge of desire that her voice invoked.

"I've left Sanchez's office," Nicole said. "I'm on my way to talk to Dad. Carlos says if Dad keeps poking at things he's only going to make it worse."

"I think it'll be good for you to spend a little time with your father, Nicole. You aren't due for a scene until tonight."

"Yes, the fire scene," Nicole said. "Actually, this is my favorite. Do you think Familiar will balk at the fire? Most animals don't like it."

"I think he'll do just fine. To be honest, I think he understands a lot more than Angela or Kyle about how to be a professional actor."

Nicole's soft laughter was like a sensuous finger dancing along his spine. Jax had the strongest impulse to stop everything he was doing and to go to her, to pull her into his arms.

"I would never underestimate that cat," she said. "Watching him work that scene this morning was the best. Did you ever hear what happened with Angela?''

''Gossip on the set is that she's taken to bed with a sick headache. She refuses to see anyone, even John Hudson.''

''Jax, is there something going on with John?'' Nicole asked. ''He asked me to lunch, then canceled. That doesn't sound like him.''

''I know. But he gave me no hint what was going on in his head.''

''Is he getting ready to fire me? I mean the cops have been out to the set twice. Once I was arrested and the second time I was questioned. That doesn't look good.''

''And you did nothing wrong either time,'' Jax assured her. ''John is conscious of how a bad buzz can wreck a movie, but he isn't a superstitious fool. I would suspect that if he wanted to fire anyone, it would be Angela. She's the source of all this trouble, not you.''

''But he can't fire Angela, and he certainly can replace me.''

''Not if I have anything to say. Besides, I don't even think he's considering such a thing. John acted distracted, not upset.''

Nicole's sigh was whisper soft. ''I listen to you and you soothe me.''

''I'm glad,'' he said. He knew what a big step it was for Nicole to admit such a thing.

''I just can't let myself think about what I'm going to do when I don't have you. This movie will end in a few weeks. You'll go on to your next job, and I'll see what I have left when the dust settles in my life.''

''What if we work together again? I have another movie lined up and you'd be perfect for the female stunts.'' He knew better than to offer more than that. Nicole had opened the door to their future. He had to step forward inch by inch. If Nicole thought he was offering more, she'd distrust him and bolt. He surprised himself that he wanted to offer more.

''Another movie?''

He heard the hope in her voice and his heart thudded with excitement.

''We'll talk about it tonight. Tell your father I said hello.''

''I'll do that,'' she said.

''Nicole, you never did tell me what the curse of the Dream of Isis is.''

There was a pause before she spoke again. ''It's said that whoever touches the diamond will lose his dream. The stone is supposed to absorb the dreams of each individual who holds it, and that's why it burns with such fire.''

Jax felt as if a cool breeze had suddenly blown across his skin. ''That's a pretty terrible curse.''

''And I fear it may be true,'' she said. ''That stone has brought nothing but tragedy to my family.''

''Perhaps it's best if it remains lost.''

''The only good thing about finding it would be to clear my father's name.''

''Then we'll do our best to find it and return it to Richard Weeks.''

"But it doesn't belong to him. I'm not certain, but I think it belongs to an insurance company now."

Jax felt as if he'd been poleaxed. He should have realized that. Most of the jewels worn on Oscar night belonged to jewelry companies, but they were all insured. If the company had paid out a claim on the stone, then they now owned it. "Who does own the stone?" he asked.

"I was never certain."

"Be sure and ask your father, please. This could be very important."

"If Dad doesn't know, I'm sure it's in the case file, which I got from Carlos Sanchez."

"I can't wait to have a look at that."

"I'll give you a call when I get back on the set," Nicole said before she hung up.

Jax slipped the cell phone back in its case just as he felt a tap on his shoulder. He turned around slowly and felt a flash of pain as Angela's hand met his face.

"You bastard," she said. "I don't know how you did it, but you set that whole thing up this morning with those jewels."

She drew back to slap him again, but Jax caught her wrist and held it firmly. "I wouldn't do that again, Angela," he said calmly.

"Let me go," she said through clenched teeth.

"I will, but I'm telling you, if you slap me again I'll hog-tie you right here in the dirt." He released her wrist and waited. She was smarter than he thought, because she took a step back from him.

"Thanks to you the police were all over me this

morning. I didn't get a bit of sleep. Now I have a scene and I look like crap.''

She was a bit worn, but the makeup artists would soon have her luminous. ''I don't know why you're blaming me, Angela. The better question is what was Monica's broach doing in your trailer.''

''Not in my trailer, you Texas buffoon, under it! There's a big difference. And how did you get that damn cat to drag it out like that?''

''You give me far too much credit if you think I can train a cat to do anything.'' He fought to hide the smile that threatened to sneak across his face. ''In fact, I think Familiar and Elvis would be very put out with the idea that they would lower themselves to perform tricks.''

''You're nuts, and you're a sicko to boot,'' Angela said. ''All of you act like those cats think and feel. It's ridiculous.''

Out of the corner of his eye, Jax saw Familiar in the shade of a tree. The cat was listening intently—and with a peculiar glint in his eye.

''What were you doing with Monica's broach?'' Jax asked, changing the subject abruptly. He hoped he could trip Angela up.

''I don't have to answer your questions.''

''No, you don't,'' Jax said. ''But it does look very suspicious, Angela. First you lose an earring, for which you immediately point the finger of blame at Nicole. It's found in her trailer. When Monica's jewelry goes missing, Nicole is once again a suspect.

But this time the broach is found in your possession."

"It was under my trailer. How many times do I have to say that? It wasn't exactly in my possession. Anyone could have put it there."

"How does it feel to be accused of something?" he pressed. "Not very good. So before you go pointing the finger of blame at Nicole, maybe you should remember how this feels."

"I don't have to listen to your lectures," she huffed as she started to walk away. "I have work to do. You and that sticky-fingered blonde had better stay out of my way."

"Or what?" Jax asked. "You make threats all the time, Angela. I'm curious to find out if they're all as empty as your head or if you really are capable of doing something."

Angela stopped and swung around to face him fully. "They aren't empty, Jax. And I fear you're about to find that out the hard way."

She stormed away from him.

Jax was watching her retreat when Jason came up to his elbow. "Wow, she was hot about something."

"Angela's always hot about something."

"She sure hates Nicole. I wonder why?"

"I have no idea," Jax answered.

"Missile at four o'clock," Jason said, falling back on a military alert. "I'm out of here before we both get torpedoed."

He was as good as his word. Jax turned to confront

another angry woman, this one dark and beautiful and just as mad.

"I hear you had those two cats playing fetch with my broach this morning," Monica Kane said as she walked up to him. "Thanks to you, the police have confiscated my heirloom broach. I'd like for you to retrieve it for me. Now would be a good time."

"Be happy to, if I could. But I can't." Jax was about fed up with the prima donnas.

"I'll speak to John about this."

"Help yourself," Jax said. "John will laugh in your face. I can't help it that the police took your broach in. I'm sure they'll return it as soon as they're finished with it."

"I want it now."

Jax shook his head. "Good luck, Monica. It's not my problem."

"But Nicole Paul is your problem, isn't she?"

There was a malicious glint in Monica's eyes. Jax decided that the best thing he could do would be to confront Monica on the spot.

"What is it with you and Nicole? Why do you dislike her so much?"

"She's a Paul. And she goes around telling everyone her father is innocent."

"She believes he is."

"And I believe he ruined my career, and to a large degree, my life."

"You didn't have a hand in it at all, did you?"

"What is that supposed to mean?"

Jax shook his head. "I couldn't begin to explain it to you, Monica."

"Don't you dare get that condescending tone with me."

"Then don't act like a victim," Jax· countered. He saw the hot flame of rage jump into her cheeks. He hadn't intended to antagonize her, but he found that almost everything he said annoyed her.

"Let me tell you something, Jax McClure. You think you know Nicole, just like I thought I knew her father. You think she just needs one good break, one person to believe in her. I felt the same way about Vincent. I saw what talent he had and I arranged—by pulling strings and calling in markers— *I* arranged for Vincent to get the lion's share of the Academy jewelry work. And then he stole that diamond and I was ruined."

Jax gave Monica a contemplative look. It was possible that she was lying about arranging for Vincent to get the commissions. Neither Vincent nor Nicole had mentioned them. It was also possible that they hadn't known or that Monica had a tainted memory of history. It wasn't impossible that she'd inflated her role in her own mind.

"Monica, how did you manage to get the Dream of Isis for the Awards?"

"Funny you should ask," she said. "My former husband. Richard Weeks owned the diamond. He loaned it to me for the Oscars. Of course, he wasn't my husband then. It was shortly after that that we were married."

Jax listened to her words, but it was the bitterness on her face that told the real story. She'd married a wealthy Realtor, which explained the sudden breakup of her relationship with John Hudson.

Jax didn't believe in curses or mojos, but it did seem as if the Dream of Isis was a jewel that seemed to bring bad luck into a person's life, if Monica was any example.

"I'm sorry," he said.

"You're sorry and my life took a turn that can only be described as a road trip through hell. And that old crook Vincent is out of jail and still has the diamond."

Jax raised his eyebrows. "You believe he still has it?"

"Of course he does. A stone that size doesn't simply disappear. He's the only one who could have it. His shop wasn't robbed. The police said they found scratches on the back door that might indicate a break-in. That type of thing is easy enough to set up. But Vincent's safe was opened by someone who knew the combination."

"And how many people knew the combination?"

"As far as I know only Vincent." She hesitated. "And myself."

"You knew how to open the safe?" Jax was surprised.

"Vincent gave me the proper sequence. In case anything happened to him I'd be able to get the diamond out."

Jax contained his excitement. It was the first inkling he'd had that someone else might have been able to access Vincent's safe. "Monica, did you memorize the combination to the safe?"

"Don't be ridiculous. I didn't have to memorize it."

"What do you mean?"

"It was coded so that it was something I'd never forget. Something that I would always remember."

Jax took a deep breath. "What was the code?"

Monica gave him a withering look. "I don't suppose it matters now. The combination to the safe was based on my social security number. Vincent set it up that way to make sure I'd always be able to open the safe. It was fifty-five left, sixty-eight right, seventy-three left, ninety-four right, and six left."

When Jax didn't say anything, Monica continued. "I thought it was terribly clever. Until Vincent betrayed me. I'll never forgive him. Or his daughter. Every time I see Nicole I think of her father. She's nothing more than a galling reminder."

"Enough of a reminder that you'd conspire with Angela Myers to try and set her up as a thief?"

"I don't know what you're talking about, and I resent the implication that I'd set anyone up."

"The broach that went missing—you didn't give it to Angela?"

Monica rolled her eyes. "I don't care for Nicole, but I don't like Angela either. I have no use for either of them. In fact, I don't even know why I agreed to take part in this silly film. John has lost his grip on fine filmmaking. I wish I'd never come here."

She turned around and left, leaving Jax with a whir of possibilities racing through his brain.

NICOLE PARKED her car in the steep drive to her father's house. His old battered Volvo was parked beneath a tree, and she noticed that leaves had drifted on top of it. So her father was staying home. Before he'd gone to prison, he'd been up at the crack of dawn to have breakfast at the diner with some of his friends. Now she couldn't help but wonder if those same old friends would agree to meet him. He was a convicted felon. That word left a metallic taste in her mouth and a tear in her heart.

She knocked loudly on the door and when there was no answer, she tried the knob. To her surprise it was unlocked. Vincent wasn't a careless man. He'd always taken care to lock doors and windows. She pushed the door open and stepped into the house.

The first thing she noticed was the smell. Something was very wrong. Instead of the lemony odor of cleaners and furniture polish, there was the delicious smell of seafood. Her body tensed for action as she moved into the house.

She considered calling out to her father but decided against it. She didn't want to startle him, but she also didn't want to alert anyone else who might be in the house, and she was certain that something was wrong.

She moved into the kitchen and saw the mess. She could read the telltale signs as easily as if they'd been written on cue cards. Vincent had been preparing dinner. Something with a red sauce. The half-shelled shrimp were still in the colander in the sink, and the sauce on the stove.

Several broken dishes were on the floor and two chairs were overturned.

Her heartbeat increased until she could hear the blood drumming in her ears. There had been violence in her father's house.

She suppressed the impulse to run through the rooms screaming his name. It would do no good and it might only make matters worse. She had to keep her head, to move slowly and silently. If she should come upon whoever had her father, she might be able to surprise them.

She left the kitchen and silently slipped through the upper rooms, at last descending down to her father's bedroom. She was almost afraid of what she might find when she pushed open the door to his room. To her relief, the room was empty.

The bed was made, as if Vincent had never gone to bed the night before. Nothing was out of place. All of the action had taken place on the upper floor, around dinnertime.

Since the house was empty there was no need for quiet. She ran up the stairs and into the kitchen. She took in every detail of the scene. There was no blood, nothing to indicate that her father had been hurt. But he had been abducted, she was certain of that.

She flipped out her cell phone and dialed Jax. He answered almost immediately.

"Someone's kidnapped Dad," she said, hearing how close to an emotional breakdown she was. She swallowed. "I'd say they got him around seven last night. Jax, what am I going to do?"

Chapter Eleven

Jax took the curves to Vincent Paul's house at high speed but with great care. Beside him, Familiar perched on the front seat of the truck, his claws stabilizing him on the sharper turns.

Focusing on his driving, Jax was able to keep his mind from the dire possibilities of what might have happened to Nicole's father. There would be time enough to deal with that when he had a look at the abduction scene.

He'd urged Nicole not to call the police. Not yet. He wanted a chance to read the clues before he turned the scene over to the authorities. There was no doubt Vincent's abduction went back to the Dream of Isis. Police officials viewed that case as closed, so it would be difficult to convince them otherwise. Jax knew it was up to him, Nicole and Familiar to figure it out.

And time was of vital importance.

He pulled into the drive and parked behind Nicole's car. It was half past four in the afternoon. If

Nicole's estimate of the time Vincent was taken was accurate, he'd been gone almost twenty-four hours.

So far no ransom note.

He knew that didn't bode well, but there was always the chance it was in the house and had been overlooked.

The front door flew open and Nicole hurtled across the yard.

"He didn't take his heart medication!" Tears ran down her cheeks.

Jax pulled her into his arms, holding her as she sobbed. Nicole wasn't a woman who broke down. He knew the best thing he could do for her would be to give her a job, something to make her feel she was helping her father.

"Good work, Nicole. Now, did you find anything else?" He had to focus her on finding her father, not on what might have happened to Vincent.

She shook her head. "I looked through the kitchen, the bedroom and the bath. I didn't find anything. They just took him."

"There's nothing out of the ordinary? No clue or hint?" So intense was Jax in comforting Nicole that he didn't notice Familiar slip into the house.

"Nothing," Nicole said, working hard to gather her raw emotions.

"We'll look again," Jax said. "There's bound to be something. I found out a very interesting tidbit from Monica Kane. She had the code to Vincent's safe. The combination was her social security number."

Nicole's eyes widened. "Then anyone who had access to her social security number and knew it was the combination to the safe could have opened the safe."

"Exactly," Jax said, his lips a grim line. "Any accountant, payroll office, law enforcement official, immigration official, police officer, employer—the list goes on and on. And Monica wasn't even aware how damning this information is, which is an indication she might have accidentally told someone."

"I don't think my father considered how dangerous this could be," Nicole said softly. "As he told you, his father emigrated and was then killed. Dad was so proud to be an American. I doubt it ever crossed his mind that anyone other than good people would be able to get such personal information."

"But we have a direction," Jax said, relieved that Nicole was thinking. As someone who seldom let his emotions get out of control, Jax knew how difficult it was to pull back from that brink. "That's the most important thing. At least now we have something to follow. And I have no doubt, Nicole, that this is the path that will lead us to your father."

"If he's still alive," she said, her voice wavering and breaking at the last.

Jax gently grasped her chin and forced her to look into his eyes. "He's alive. Don't doubt it. Vincent is alive and certain that we'll help him. Your father may have a heart condition, but he's a tough old bird. Remember that."

"He doesn't have his medicine. And what if he's hurt." Nicole's eyes filled.

"There's no sign of blood in the house, no reason to even think that." He knew he might be wrong, but he had to give Nicole hope that her father was safe. "Let's just go on the assumption that your father is valuable to them only if he's alive and able to talk. They want the diamond. They think he knows where it is. He can't help them if he's sick or injured."

He saw his reasoning take hold in Nicole's mind. Her jaw lifted and her shoulders squared. His already high opinion of her inched up several notches. She was incredibly brave.

"Let's get to work," she said. "We have to find Dad."

THE SCENE in the yard is highly charged with emotion, but Jax can handle it without my help. I think my skills can best be employed by taking a look around this house.

Nicole said there were no clues, but she doesn't have the keen eyesight of a feline. And she hasn't been trained in the art of being a private dick. I could mention that she is an inferior species, but that kind of comment isn't seemly under these conditions. Not to mention that it's highly uncharitable.

For a humanoid, Nicole's on the really bright side. I truly don't understand all of the jokes bipeds tell about blondes. Nicole is quite intelligent. Then on the other hand, Angela is blond, too. Hmmm. This issue deserves further study. But at a later date, when I'm at my leisure instead of on a case.

I'm scanning the door of Vincent's house. There's no sign of forced entry. Either the door was un-latched when the kidnappers arrived or he let them in. Because they were armed or, perhaps, because he knew them. To be determined later.

The kitchen shows some type of struggle. Nicole hasn't touched anything, so I can walk around and try to visualize what happened. I think I'll take my vantage point from the counter rather than the floor. Cat perspective is another plus for detecting. We can look at things from high, low and middle ground. Humans often forget to do this.

Judging from the evidence inside the house, I'd say Vincent welcomed his guests into the house. That in-dicates it was someone he knew and felt safe around, or at least unthreatened by. As I visualize the sce-nario based on the evidence, it would seem Vincent returned to the sink and resumed peeling the shrimp he was preparing for his dinner. The red sauce had been made, and the pot of water to boil the pasta was already on the stove.

There's a half glass of wine on the counter. Hmmm, smells like a good, tart white to complement the shrimp. But only one glass, so he didn't offer his guests a drink, or else they declined.

I'd guess that whoever was in the house grabbed Vincent while he was still at the sink. He struggled against them and kicked over the chairs in the pro-

cess. He was overpowered and dragged out of the house and taken.

Aha! There's a dull scuffmark on the tile floor in the entry area. That would support my theory that he was dragged outside while struggling. I think I've figured out what happened, I just don't know who took him.

The next place I want to check is the bedroom. Nicole said she didn't think anyone had been in there, but it never hurts to be extra careful. I'm just glad Nicole didn't panic and call the cops. We'd never be able to take our time with the crime scene like this if the police were here. I've found it difficult to work with the law. Well, I am a cat and they do find that more than a little unbelievable.

The bedroom looks undisturbed at first glance. I see where Nicole found Vincent's heart medicine on the bedside table. I would have thought he'd keep it in the bathroom medicine cabinet. Let me check there a moment. Nothing unusual, just the regular shaving things, aspirin and toothpaste.

Back to the bedroom. Odd, Vincent doesn't have an answering machine. I suppose he didn't expect to get a lot of messages since he just got out of prison. On the other hand, he could have one of those answering services. I'll bet Nicole hasn't thought to check that.

Let's just flip the phone off the charger, hit Talk and there it is, the stutter signal that says there's a call. This phone is awkward to carry, but I've got to get it to Nicole and Jax. The message on here could be from the kidnapper!

I've made it up the stairs, and here they come in from the yard.

"Me-ow!" *That got their attention.*

Nicole has caught on fast. She has the telephone and is listening to the little stutter sound. She knows what it means and her brown eyes have lit with hope. Please, please, let this be some clue to Vincent's whereabouts! I sure would hate to let her down.

Dang! She doesn't know the code to collect his calls. Where would he hide such a thing? He's a man. An artistic man. Let me think. Based on my dealings with artistes, I'd say the numbers would be somewhere easy to find. Vincent hasn't been out of prison for long, so he might need to prompt his memory. And the logical place would be right beside the phone.

There wasn't a pad by the bedroom phone, but there is one here by the kitchen extension. And there the numbers are!

"Meow! Meow!"

Nicole is dialing. She's holding the phone so that Jax and I both can hear, along with her.

Oh my goodness. It's Vincent's voice. This is the clue. He left it here for Nicole to find.

"Nicole, this is your father. I'm in grave danger. Whatever you do, don't call the police. The men who have me want the Dream of Isis. They insist that I know where it is. You must find that stone if you want to see me alive again. I need my heart medica—'' *The line has gone dead.*

I don't think Nicole is going to faint, but she sure is pale. That's right, Jax, get her in a chair. Let me find some brandy or something. She needs a little fortification. And to that end, so do I. I always want to eat when I'm upset. Comfort food. Like poached salmon over wild rice. I have to say, as soon as Vincent is back home safe and sound, I'm going to demand dinner at the finest restaurant in Los Angeles.

Now we have to decide what to do next.

NICOLE ACCEPTED the glass of whiskey Jax handed her. She took a sip and let the burn warm her inside, but she still felt icy cold. Her father had been abducted and he needed his medication. She knew that was the message he was trying to get to her. What was she going to do?

"Shall we call the police?" she asked Jax.

"I don't think that would be wise," he said slowly. "Nicole, I believe your father is perfectly fine as long as we don't do anything rash." Jax chose not to mention anything about heart medication.

"He doesn't have that diamond, and neither do I. What are we going to do?"

"Did you bring the case file?"

"It's in my car."

"Let me get it and we'll take a look at it. There has to be something we can go on."

"Jax, if my father doesn't take his medicine on a

regular basis, his heart could seize and stop. The doctor was very specific about this danger.''

''Meow!'' Familiar batted the bottle of medicine, knocking it to the floor. In a moment he'd knocked it into Nicole's shoe.

''I know,'' Nicole said, picking it up and squeezing it in her hand until her knuckles whitened. ''I know, Familiar. I only wish I could get it to him.''

''I'll be right back. Sip the whiskey,'' Jax directed as he went out to the car. He returned a few moments later with the case file. He hadn't had a chance to look at it, but it was suspiciously thin. He'd been expecting a lot more material.

Jax, Nicole and Familiar took the file into the den, using the coffee table as their base to open the file and begin an examination.

''I'll read the trial transcript,'' Nicole said.

''I'll take the police reports.''

''What are we looking for?'' Nicole asked, turning to face Jax.

She was so worried and upset, he had to think of something logical and real. He couldn't admit to her that he wasn't certain what they were hunting. He could only hope that something would strike him as odd.

''Check Monica's testimony. See if she mentions about having the code.''

When Nicole was busy, he began to leaf through the police reports. Most of them contained only the information that Jax knew already.

He felt a slight bump on his shoe and looked down

to find that Familiar had batted Vincent's medicine bottle across the room. He leaned down to pick it up. Seeing it again would only upset Nicole more.

He picked up the reports again. Suddenly he felt razor sharp claws in his leg.

"Familiar!" he said, reaching under the table for the cat. "Let go."

"Me-ow!" Familiar released his leg but jumped on the coffee table. In one swift leap he was across the table onto the sofa and digging into the cushions where Jax had stowed the prescription bottle. In a moment he had it out, batting it across the floor.

"What's wrong with him?" Nicole asked.

"I don't know." Jax reached for the bottle again. He held it up for the cat. Familiar gently placed his paw on it, patting it a couple of times.

"He's trying to tell us something, I just don't know what," Jax said, frustrated by his inability to figure out what the cat was trying to do.

Nicole took the bottle from him and looked at it. She read the prescription number, the directions, the doctor's name, the number of refills left.

Jax watched as her eyes opened. "It's the refills," she said. "That's what he's trying to tell us. Dad will have to get the prescription refilled."

Jax swiftly rose to his feet. "Exactly. That's why he left the medicine. That's what he was trying to tell us about his medication. He was hinting to us and Familiar was the only one who figured it out."

"Where is Rexall One Stop?" Nicole asked, using the name of the pharmacy where the prescription had been filled. "He'll have to go back there or call his doctor."

"You call the doctor, I'll call the pharmacy on my cell phone," Jax said. "If they haven't picked up the prescription yet, maybe we can catch them."

"Or maybe we should call the police now," Nicole said. "I'm afraid for my dad."

"Meow!" Familiar said with great emphasis.

"Is that a no?"

Familiar blinked, nodding his head.

"The cat is against calling the cops," Jax pointed out, "and I tend to agree with him. I think we should continue on our own."

"Let's make those calls and then see."

Jax used his cell phone as he watched Nicole's face for any shift of expression.

When he had the pharmacist on the phone, he focused all of his attention on what he was doing. At first the pharmacist was reluctant to give any information, until Jax explained that Vincent needed his heart medication and they were trying to make sure he had gotten it filled.

"You can rest easy," the pharmacist finally said, "Mr. Paul came by for his prescription not ten minutes ago. He looked fine."

"I see," Jax said, trying to hide his excitement. "Was he alone?"

"Seemed to be. But he wasn't his normal talkative self. I'm glad to know he has someone looking out for him like you are."

"Did he happen to leave a new address of any kind?"

There was a pause. "What's this about?" the pharmacist asked.

"It's a long story, but you have to believe we have only his best interest at heart."

Something in Jax's voice must have convinced the pharmacist. "Mr. Paul came in alone. He seemed distracted, and he did keep looking out the drive-through window, as if he expected to see someone. That's all I can tell you."

"Did he pay with cash or a check?"

"I believe it was a check. Why?"

"I'll be there with his daughter as soon as I can." Jax hung up and he didn't have to ask how Nicole had fared. Her face told it all—she hadn't met with any success.

"Dad didn't call his doctor at all."

"No, he got it refilled at the pharmacy, but we have a small lead there. Your father paid by check."

"What kind of lead is that?"

"We'll have to look at the check to find out."

Nicole's face broke into a smile. "Brilliant, Jax. Dad may have tried to leave us a message on his check."

"We can at least look."

"I hope so because I don't see a thing in the transcript."

"The police files are pretty slim, too. I think there must have been additional reports, but someone's taken them."

"Carlos warned me that older files often aren't well maintained. I shouldn't have expected more," Nicole said, battling against her fear and disappointment.

"Let's go," Jax said, opening the front door. He needed to get her out of the house.

"What about Familiar?" Nicole asked.

"He's our best investigator. We're not about to leave him behind."

Chapter Twelve

"This is highly irregular," Joe Evans said as he opened the cash drawer in the pharmacy.

"I'm his daughter," Nicole said. She had to convince the pharmacist to let her look at the check. So far, it was the only lead they had to Vincent's whereabouts—if it *was* a lead. "I have identification. More than that, I have a good reason. I just want to look at the check."

Joe Evans assessed her and then turned to Jax. "What's going on here?"

"My father may be in trouble," Nicole said. "He may have written something on the back of the check, hoping that I'd think to look." Normally she would have fought the tears that began to well in her eyes, but now she let them.

Joe frowned at her. "This sounds like some kind of joke, and I'm telling the two of you, if you're wasting my time or trying to pull something, I'm not going to like it."

"Mr. Paul may be in serious trouble," Jax said. "We're telling the truth."

"I can confirm this by calling the police?" Joe asked.

"No. We can't involve the police." Jax put his arm around Nicole. "We don't want to tell you more. It's best that you know as little as possible, but please believe us. This could be a life-or-death matter."

Joe hesitated, his hand in the cash drawer. "I'm not certain I should get involved in this."

"We only want to *look* at the check," Nicole said. "Please! How will you feel if you deny us and then something happens to my father?"

"Or just look at the check yourself," Jax suggested. "If there's nothing on it, we'll leave."

"That sounds reasonable," Joe said reluctantly. He went through a stack of checks until he found the one he wanted. When he turned it over, he froze. "We'll I'll be," he said. Without another word he handed the check over to Nicole.

She moved so that Jax could examine the message with her.

"It's a phone number," Jax said as he wrote it down on a piece of paper on the counter. He handed the check back to the pharmacist. "Thanks, Mr. Evans."

"Do you think it's important?" Joe Evans asked.

"It's hard to tell," Nicole said.

"You're welcome to use the telephone," the pharmacist said, nodding at it. Now that evidence had been presented he was far more cooperative.

"I think it would be best if we could figure out

who the number belongs to before we call it," Jax suggested.

"Let me give you a word of advice," Joe said. "You should contact the police. Whatever is wrong, they're the people who can help you fix it."

"I'm not so certain of that," Nicole said. "I wish it were true."

"I knew who your father was when he was on top of the world. He was a young man, and so was I. He didn't take medicine, but sometimes he would stop in to get a few things. We weren't friends, but we were friendly. I never believed he was a thief," Joe said. "I can understand why you're reluctant to call the authorities. But do it. I urge you. If there's foul play afoot, and there certainly does seem to be, the police are the ones who can help you."

Nicole took a deep breath. "Thanks for your concern, Mr. Evans. And for your help. I'll think about what you've said, but right now, I can't risk it."

"Is there anyone in the store who might have seen Vincent get in or out of a car?" Jax asked.

Joe's eyebrows rose. "Maybe Lenny. He was out changing the letters on the sign. I'll get him."

Nicole paced the small area in front of the pharmacy as she waited for Joe to return with the gangly teenager.

"Tell them what you saw," Joe prompted the kid.

"It was a black car. Real nice. I don't know what kind. Big, though. And the dude in the turtleneck got out of the back and went in the store. Then he came out and got back in the back seat. That's all I know."

"Was there anyone in the car except the driver?" Nicole asked.

"Yeah, there was another guy in the passenger seat. I guess it was a guy. The windows were tinted pretty dark, so I couldn't see inside real good."

"Make, model, license plate?" Jax pressed.

Lenny shook his head. "Sorry. It was just a big, clean, black car. Luxury type. I didn't notice anything else."

"You did good," Jax told him. "Thanks."

"Why did you notice the car at all?" Nicole asked.

"It made me think of movies where the bad guys sort of hover outside a place. And the dude in the turtleneck looked like an actor. You know, real cool." He shrugged.

"Thanks, Lenny," Nicole said. She'd hoped for something extra, some little detail.

"Oh, yeah," Lenny said. "There was one thing. The car had some kind of parking thing hanging in the front window. It was orange and green. An orange P on a green background."

Nicole felt her hopes rise. "That's great, Lenny. Thank you."

"You folks had better go outside and get your cat, though. He jumped out the window of your truck and he was walking around the parking lot."

"We'd better go," Jax said, taking Nicole's elbow. "Thank you both."

They hurried outside and hesitated as they scanned

the parking lot for Familiar. There was no sign of the black cat.

In a moment, Nicole spotted him. "There!" she pointed. "He's got something."

She didn't need to say anything further. Jax trotted off, headed straight for the cat.

Nicole was right on Jax's heels, and in a moment she had Familiar scooped into her arms while Jax examined the slip of paper the cat had speared with his claws.

"It's a laundry receipt," Jax said. "Elmwood Laundry in Sherman Oaks."

"It could have come out of any vehicle," Nicole pointed out.

"Me-ow!" Familiar shook his head.

"I don't think so. Cats have an uncanny sense of smell," Jax reminded her. "I think Familiar would be able to tell if Vincent touched this."

"Meow!" Familiar said in what sounded like an agreement.

"What about the phone number?"

"We can call Information and see if they'll give us the name that matches it."

"Let's get on it." Nicole carried Familiar in her arms as they got in the truck. In a moment Jax had information on his cell phone.

He listened to the operator and then hung up. "It's an unlisted number. They won't release the name."

"Damn!" Nicole said. "That's our best lead. Other than that we've got a laundry ticket."

"Then that's what we're going to have to pursue,"

Jax said as he started the truck and drove toward the exclusive neighborhood of Sherman Oaks.

THERE'S NO DOUBT in my mind that Vincent Paul touched this laundry stub, but did he simply knock it out of the car as he was getting out? I have no way of knowing his intent. This is the frustration of all investigators. Evidence tells only so much—the rest is instinct, experience and a knowledge of human nature.

I scouted the entire parking lot and didn't find another clue. But my gut tells me that Vincent is doing everything he can to leave us a trail. He's pretty crafty for a jeweler.

The phone number is our best chance of finding him. It's a deliberate clue. But it's also going to be the hardest to track. At this point, I'm beginning to wonder if Nicole should go to the police. It wouldn't take them a minute to get the proper listing to match the number.

But we can check out the laundry stub first. And then we should check the voice mail for Vincent again. He may have called with more specific information.

At the bottom of all of this is the Dream of Isis. The stone still hasn't been recovered. My thinking on this is that the people holding Vincent really believe he has it. That means someone else actually has the stone. Someone who was never suspected. Someone who values the stone for reasons other than displaying it. I somehow have to make Jax and Nicole follow this line of thinking. It's the path that will eventually lead us to the Dream of Isis.

"JAX, WHAT ABOUT the shoot we have tonight?" Nicole asked, glancing at her watch. The afternoon was slipping away from them. "John will fire you if you don't show up. He'll fire me, too. That's of no importance, but you have a career to consider."

"Maybe not."

"What do you mean?"

"This scene is the one with Monica Kane, right?"

"Yes."

Jax could see the puzzlement on her face as he glanced over at her. He couldn't resist taking her hand. He gave it a light squeeze. "I don't think we'll be missed if Monica Kane is also missing."

Nicole's smile was a million watts. "And just why should Monica Kane be missing from the set tonight?"

"Because she wants revenge for what she perceives as the destruction of her career."

"True, but how is she going to achieve that?"

"By helping us find that diamond," Jax said. "I've given it a lot of thought, and that stone is somewhere nearby. I can feel it."

"I've always felt it hadn't traveled far," Nicole said.

"Think about it. Your father hasn't been out of prison for even a month, and someone has been after him almost from day one."

"They even tried to use setting me up to pressure him into revealing the diamond's whereabouts."

"But Vincent never had the stone. And the only person we haven't heard from in all of this is the original owner."

"Richard Weeks," Nicole said. She picked up the case file from the floorboard of the truck. "His address is in these documents."

"What was his testimony at the trial?" Jax asked.

"Let me find it again," she said as she began to shuffle through the papers.

As Jax drove, Nicole read the passages from the trial transcript that contained Richard Weeks's testimony.

"Basically all he says is that he loaned the diamond to Monica Kane in good faith," Jax said.

"And that he approved the security measures at the store," Nicole said.

"But the diamond was insured," Jax said. "Weeks received the value of the stone when it was stolen."

"Yes, but to some people, money wouldn't be an adequate replacement for a showpiece like the Dream of Isis."

"You have a good point. And his address is in the transcript?"

"Right."

"We'll be in that neighborhood anyway. I think we should pay Richard Weeks a visit." Jax grinned. "It would also be the perfect place from which to give Monica a little call."

"I like the way you think," Nicole said. "For the first time since I found Dad was missing I'm beginning to have some hope that we may find him."

"You can't lose hope, Nicole. You father is only useful to them alive. And he's a smart man. Very smart. Look at all the clues he's left us. He hasn't given up hope and neither can you."

"I guess I should take it as a good sign that whoever has him let him refill his medicine."

"A very good sign. And think, they let him go into the pharmacy alone. They're pretty sure he isn't going to try to escape. So we should take that to mean he isn't afraid for his life."

"I hadn't thought of that," Nicole said.

"We're nipping at their heels. I can feel it. We just need a break and a little more time."

"Me-ow!" Familiar chimed in.

NICOLE TAPPED her nails impatiently on the counter of the dry cleaner, putting on the airs of an exasperated woman of wealth.

"Here it is," the young woman behind the counter said with some relief. She came forward with a plastic wrapped suit. "Shall I put it on Mr. Sanchez's account?"

For a moment the name stunned Nicole. "Yes, that would be perfectly fine," she said, recovering and reaching for the suit.

"Is there anything else I can do for you?" the young woman asked with a curious look on her face.

"You aren't the usual person who brings Mr. Sanchez's laundry. Where's Elisabeth?"

"She was ill today," Nicole lied with aplomb.

"I hope she feels better," the clerk said, watching Nicole closely. "Excuse me, but could I see some identification."

Nicole realized then that she'd overstayed her welcome. "I don't have time," she said, snatching the suit and hurrying out of the shop. She was getting in the truck and slamming the door when she saw the clerk at the window, telephone in hand.

"Make tracks," she told Jax. "I think that young woman is reporting us to the police for suit theft."

Jax didn't waste time asking questions. He drove into the flow of traffic, his eye on the rearview mirror.

"I don't think she could get the tag number," he said.

"I hope not. We have enough trouble."

"So who did the suit belong to?" Jax asked. Beside him Familiar was patting Nicole's leg with a paw.

"Carlos Sanchez." She watched the same expression of puzzlement and then concern cross Jax's face.

"Meow?" Familiar's tone was a question.

"Do you think Dad meant for me to call Carlos?"

Jax shook his head. "That's a tough one." He stroked the cat's black fur. "Familiar, are you sure that ticket was left by Vincent?"

"Meow!" Familiar was adamant.

"Then we have to assume that he intended for us

to follow up on it somehow.'' Jax began to slow as they turned down a street lined with palm trees and exclusive homes.

"I just don't know. I spoke with Carlos this afternoon and all he did was tell me to keep Dad out of my legal problems.'' She felt her panic begin to build anew.

"Steady, Nicole,'' Jax said as he found the address he was seeking. "We have to put up the correct image for Mr. Weeks.''

"Of course,'' she said. "What about Familiar?''

"I think we should leave Familiar to his own devices. While we're talking with Mr. Weeks, I'll bet Familiar can do a bit of investigating. You did tell me he's a private eye, remember?''

Nicole nodded and found a weak smile for Jax. "What would I do without you, Jax?''

"Meow!''

"And you, too, Familiar,'' she said, scratching the cat's chin. "Once we get Dad back, I'm going to buy you the finest seafood platter this town has to offer.''

"And what am *I* going to get?'' Jax asked.

The hungry note in his voice sent shock waves through her. "Whatever you want,'' she said, her voice breathless. "Anything I have.''

Jax stopped the truck in front of an elegant home. "I know what I want from you, Nicole. And it isn't just a passing week or month of your time.''

The look in his clear blue eyes melted her heart.

"Whatever it is, I'll try not to disappoint you.''

"Nothing about you could ever disappoint me. Back in Texas, when I broke up with Sue Anne, I never thought I'd risk caring about another woman. I didn't intend to care about you. I admired you. I wanted to help you, but somewhere in all of this, I began to care for you. Now I'm afraid I may have fallen in love with you."

Nicole wanted to put her finger over his lips and stop him. These were words she'd longed to hear from Jax, but now they frightened her.

"Everyone I love gets hurt," she told him. "My mother, my father, everyone. I used to lie in my bed at night after Dad was first taken to prison and I thought that perhaps I was the one cursed. Not the diamond but me. Because it seemed that everyone I loved suffered so much."

Jax reached across and touched her face. "I don't believe in curses, Nicole. I believe in miracles, though. That's the category I'd put you in."

Nicole covered his hand with hers. "From the first moment you offered your help, you changed my life."

"I want a big change. I want a future with you. And if I'm scaring you, that's okay. We'll handle the fear together. But when we walk in that door, we walk in together."

"That's more than I ever dared hope for," she said, wiping a tear from her cheek. "Now, let's find my dad."

Chapter Thirteen

Jax was shocked that they'd been allowed to enter the home of Richard Weeks. The butler had left them in a small reception area, but he hadn't seemed at all surprised that a couple in a pickup truck had come calling on his employer.

They were still standing in front of an ornate mirror when a slender gentleman in his late fifties came toward them.

"I'm Richard Weeks, what can I do for you?" he asked. If he was curious, Jax noted that he hid it well.

Jax made the introductions and noticed the flicker of recognition in Richard's eyes when he mentioned Nicole's last name.

"Are you by chance related to Vincent Paul, the jeweler?" Richard asked.

"I'm his daughter," Nicole said.

"Then I can assume this visit has something to do with the Dream of Isis. I heard Vincent was released." He frowned. "Has he decided to reveal the whereabouts of the diamond now that he's done his time?"

"My father never had the diamond," Nicole said hotly.

Jax put a hand on her arm. "We're here about the diamond, Mr. Weeks, but not because we have it or know where it is. We're actually looking for it."

"Good luck. I had the best detectives money could buy try and track it down. It disappeared. Every indication was that Vincent Paul took the diamond and hid it. Now that he's out, I expect he'll reap the benefits of the jewel. Or perhaps the curse." His lips twisted slightly.

"Mr. Weeks," Jax said, cutting off another hot outburst from Nicole, "I have just a few questions. If you can assume for just a moment that Vincent Paul didn't take the stone, who might have done so?"

Weeks's brow furrowed. "I haven't thought of this in a long time. In my mind, Vincent had the stone. When it became apparent that he wasn't going to tell where it was hidden, I gave up on the diamond. Even so, I didn't escape the bite of the curse."

"Please think," Nicole said, her temper firmly under control. "It could be very important."

Weeks frowned. "I followed the case very closely, of course, and all the evidence pointed at Vincent. I do have to say that I was as astounded as everyone else when Monica called and told me the stone was stolen. I knew Vincent through Monica. He had her total respect and trust, and he'd also won me over."

"My father is an honorable man," Nicole interjected. "He isn't a thief."

Weeks was staring at her as he continued. "There were several jewelry designers Monica could have chosen. I followed the designs that Vincent created for the jewel and they were nothing less than spectacular."

"So you see, it doesn't make sense that my father would have stolen the jewel before Monica wore it to the Oscars. That would have been the crowning glory of my father's career. It would have been his opportunity to show to the world his creative genius."

Jax watched Weeks's face as he thought about what Nicole had said.

"I see your point, Ms. Paul. But I also saw the evidence against your father."

"You were married to Monica not too long after the diamond disappeared, weren't you?" Jax asked.

"What does that have to do with anything?" Weeks assumed an antagonistic stance once again. "My marital affairs have nothing to do with this."

"Are you sure?" Jax asked gently. "Monica was engaged to marry John Hudson."

"I assumed Monica married me because she wanted to. What do you think? That Monica Kane couldn't care for a man like me? A Realtor instead of a film genius?"

Jax knew he was walking on thin ice. Richard Weeks was a prickly man who'd obviously been badly hurt.

"That's not what I meant," Jax said. He kept his hand on Nicole's arm, squeezing it gently to keep her silent. "Before the theft of the diamond, Monica and John Hudson were a hot item in all the trade publications. Everyone anticipated that they would marry."

"Their relationship fell apart. John dumped her. He left her flat. Her career started to unravel and he didn't want her in his next film or his life. I was there when Monica needed me." Weeks's tone had grown frosty. "I still don't see what this has to do with the diamond."

"I'm not sure either. Maybe nothing," Jax conceded. "I spoke with Monica yesterday, and she said that she'd been cursed by the diamond even though she'd never owned it. What do you think she meant?"

"I have no earthly idea. Let me just say that Monica isn't the most stable person, on an emotional level, that I've ever known."

"That may be an understatement," Nicole muttered.

Jax pressed her arm once again, urging caution. "Did you happen to know Monica's connection to the code for the safe in Vincent Paul's office?" Jax continued.

"Monica's connection?" He looked puzzled. "No, I can't say that I did. What are you talking about?"

"In the evidence presented in court, only Vincent Paul had access to his shop and particularly to the safe where the diamond was kept," Jax said. "That isn't true. Monica also had access. She knew the code to the safe.''

"Monica?''

Weeks's surprise looked legitimate. Jax waited, hoping he would offer something more. ''Yes, Monica.''

"She never said anything to me.''

"I don't think she said anything to anyone. At least not knowingly. That's why we're here. To ask if you remembered anyone she might have confided in.'' Jax still hoped that Richard Weeks would reveal something.

"Why would Vincent Paul have given the code to Monica? That doesn't make sense.''

"I believe Vincent was taking a step to safeguard the stone if something happened to him. If he were ill or injured, Monica would be able to retrieve the stone and wear it.''

Richard nodded. ''I see. So Monica could have taken the stone. That's what you've come to tell me—that my ex-wife also set me up as a patsy for her international jewelry theft scam.''

Jax ignored the sarcasm, though he felt Nicole stiffen. ''I'm not saying that, Mr. Weeks. I'm not accusing Monica or anyone else. But she could have told someone else the code, either in casual conversation or thinking she could trust that person. Monica might have been deceived. Can you think of any of her friends who might be capable of something like this? Someone deceptive and very clever.''

"That would certainly cover all of her so-called

friends in the movie business. She didn't trust a single one of them. Unfortunately, none would fall under the classification of clever."

"Think about it, Mr. Weeks," Nicole said. "Please. Is there anyone you can think of who might have been a confidante of Monica's?"

"To be honest, I couldn't abide her friends. They were so catty and cruel. Everything was a competition with them. As time passed, Monica and I fought more and more about that very issue. I didn't want them in my home. They envied everything they saw and yet belittled me because I was a businessman, not an artist. Of course that didn't prevent them from swilling my liquor or turning to Monica whenever they needed rent money or a car repair."

Jax nodded. "The movie world is a difficult one, to be sure. It's next to impossible to make a living, and when people get desperate, they do unfortunate things."

"They're all insecure, and for some reason, that makes them mean. I can't abide the sort of cruelty that passes for well-intentioned criticism."

"Not everyone is like that," Nicole said.

"Perhaps not everyone. But I watched it break Monica. She had such big dreams and hopes. She was headed for the top of the mountain, and she worked hard to get there. Then it began to slip away from her. The harder she grasped it, the more elusive it became. She grew from a sensuous, loving woman into a bitter guttersnipe. She criticized everything and everyone. She was impossible to live with."

"I can see why you feel the way you do." Jax just wanted to keep him talking. Perhaps in casual conversation he'd reveal something. The other reason was that Familiar was somewhere on the grounds. What Weeks didn't reveal willingly, Familiar might discover on his own.

"The night the diamond was stolen, Monica had a fitting for her gown. She was incredibly lovely. She was twenty-eight, a woman at the peak of her young beauty and filled with potential. The critics were saying she could follow in the footsteps of Elizabeth Taylor. She was that magnificent.

"Since I was loaning her the diamond, she invited me to the fitting of the gown so I could see the entire effect. I think she knew I was smitten by her. She was involved with Hudson, and they both were supposed to stop by your father's shop to get the diamond," Weeks said.

"She was escorted by John?" Nicole asked.

"That's right. I went straight to the dress designer's shop. I was there when she arrived, her makeup ruined by tears. She was sobbing so hard I couldn't understand anything she said. When I finally did, I guess I was more worried about Monica than the stone."

Jax could easily picture the scene Weeks was giving. Glancing at Nicole out of the corner of his eye, he saw that she, too, was caught up in the story Richard Weeks was telling them.

"Monica looked at me as if all of this were my fault," Weeks said, his face twisted by the painful memory. "She said, 'It's that damn curse. It's the diamond. It's ruined me. What am I going to do?'"

For a long moment there was silence. Then Richard seemed to snap out of the power of the past. "But that has nothing to do with who stole the diamond."

"It very well may," Jax said. "That's what we're going to find out. We have to search everywhere, explore every lead. If we can find the diamond, perhaps we can give Vincent Paul the vindication he deserves."

"If you find it, don't bring it near me," Richard said.

At first Jax thought he was kidding, but as he looked at the set of Richard's jaw, he knew he was sincere. "Doesn't it belong to you?"

"I don't want it," Richard said. "I don't want it near me, and I advise you not to touch it. The damn thing is truly cursed."

"You don't really believe in the curse, do you?" Jax asked. He was surprised that someone with Richard's intelligence and world experience would admit to such a superstition.

"I didn't. I thought it was a bunch of foolishness cooked up to give the stone some mystique. Large and unusual gems always attract that type of story. Like the Hope diamond."

"And now? What do you believe now?" Nicole asked.

"That stone ruined my happiness. I can't say it ruined my life, but it did bring Monica into it, and it also took her away."

"How?"

Richard shrugged. "Her career began to slide. She changed. After a while, I just couldn't take her constant sniping and criticizing. We divorced." He gave Nicole a pensive look. "I loved Monica, but I couldn't live with her. I don't think anyone can."

"And you think that stone had something to do with that."

"You know the curse?" Richard asked. "Monica was my dream. She was the one thing I loved, the person who made everything else come to life. There were moments of sheer bliss and magic in our relationship. At first. I guess that was just preparation for the hell that would come later."

"You blame the diamond for your failed marriage?" Jax kept his voice neutral.

"The diamond destroyed Monica. *She* blamed it for the slide of her career. Whether it was true or not, she thought it was. And as her star dimmed in Hollywood, her personality became darker and more cruel."

Jax didn't know what to say.

"My father never mentioned that John Hudson was with Monica when she went to get the diamond," Nicole said, pulling the conversation onto another track.

Richard Weeks shrugged. "He was with her. That's all I know."

"Mr. Weeks, you filed an insurance claim when the diamond was stolen, correct?"

"Yes," he said. "So from that you can draw the

conclusion that should the diamond be found, it belongs to the insurance company. I certainly don't want it.''

''What company insured it?'' Jax asked.

''Regency.''

''Where are they located?'' Jax saw the company as another possible lead.

''They aren't. They haven't been in business for years. In fact, the claim I made on the diamond virtually put them out of business.''

''It would seem that the diamond *is* cursed,'' Nicole said softly. ''Everyone who touches it does suffer.''

''Some more than others. The man who owned the insurance company was destroyed. He lost everything. His business, his wife, his very existence. You can laugh about the curse if you want,'' Richard said, ''but let it suffice to say that I don't want that stone anywhere near me. I'm just not willing to take a chance. Now, if you two will excuse me, I have some things to attend to.''

''Mr. Weeks, would it be possible for me to use your telephone for just a few minutes?'' Jax's request held a note of urgency.

A frown of annoyance crossed the Realtor's features. ''I don't think so,'' he said.

''I'm sorry, my cell phone is dead and I need to make a call,'' Jax pressed.

''There's a phone in the library,'' Weeks finally agreed. ''You can use that one.''

Nicole stepped forward and asked Richard about

his business as Jax slipped into the room Weeks had indicated.

Jax listened to the soft murmur of their voices as he dialed Monica Kane's number. He'd intended to lure Monica off the movie set and Richard Weeks had given him the perfect opening. As he listened to the phone ring, he hoped Monica wouldn't be in her trailer. Luck was with him when her answering service picked up.

"Monica, this is Richard," he said in a fair imitation of the Realtor's voice. "Meet me tonight at eight at the Brown Derby. It's about the Dream of Isis and it's urgent. Don't try to call me back, just meet me there." He hung up the phone with a grim prayer that he'd sounded enough like Richard Weeks to fool Monica. The thing he had going for him was that her caller ID would show Richard's number.

I'VE ALWAYS BEEN TOLD that an organized office is the sign of a successful man. Richard Weeks fits that bill to perfection. Everything is neatly tucked away. There's not a stray piece of paper anywhere.

But that makes a search somewhat easier, now that I've figured out his filing system.

There are several photographs of the Dream of Isis, and at least I get to see the mysterious stone that's caused such problems for everyone. It is truly magnificent. Isis. Hmmm. Is that the Egyptian god of magic? I do believe so. After my recent jaunt in the deserts of Egypt, I can't help but wonder if this stone held some significance in the old rituals and traditions of the pharaohs. It wouldn't surprise me at all. If Cleopatra was once the possessor of the stone, I wonder how it got over here to Tinsel town. And following that same train wreck of a thought, just look what happened to Cleopatra.

In the file on the diamond, I've discovered the insurance payment form. Carlos Sanchez handled the legal matter of filing the claim. He took a very nice cut of the payoff. Those zeros just go on and on. I never thought one hunk of rock could hold such value. I just wonder how much the present owner paid to have it stolen from Vincent Paul's shop. I've come to the conclusion that a professional stole the jewel. Someone paid to do a job. But where is the stone residing right this minute? Who has it in his or her hot little hands?

I can't seem to find anything that gives me any leads. This is very disappointing. I'd hoped that maybe Richard Weeks was the end of the line for us, but I just don't see him as the thief. Or a kidnapper, for that matter.

I've searched this place from top to bottom and I can't find a thing that would impact our case. As much as I hate to admit it, I think we've hit another dead end here. There's no sign of Vincent anywhere in the house.

Chapter Fourteen

Nicole couldn't hide her disappointment as they left the home of Richard Weeks. She'd so hoped that she'd find her father there, even though common sense told her that such a hope had been slim.

She felt the black cat rub against her thigh and she stroked his silky fur. Familiar seemed to understand her thoughts and feelings. He was doing his best to give her comfort.

"Jax, where do you suppose my father is?" she asked.

"I don't know," he said, "but I think he's okay."

"If only we could be sure."

"Nicole, you underestimate your father. I'm developing a healthy respect for his mind and creativity. He's left us some fairly impressive clues."

"But not enough to find him."

There was a pause as Jax made a turn. When he spoke again, his voice had a completely different tone. "What did you make of the story Weeks told about Monica?"

Nicole realized Jax was deliberately attempting to

divert her from thinking about the dire things that could be happening to her father, and she felt her heart open to him. Judging him by his muscled, lean exterior, no one would ever guess how kind and sensitive he could be. Jax had no stake in what happened to her father. He'd met Vincent Paul only once. Yet Jax was risking his career and his future as a stuntman to help her. Not only to help her, but to protect her.

She slipped across the seat and gave him a kiss on the cheek. "Keep driving," she said. "I just wanted you to know how much I appreciate what you're doing."

"Meow!" Familiar demanded.

She leaned down and kissed the top of the cat's head. "And you, too, Familiar. I wouldn't leave you out."

"I should hope not," Jax said. He gave the cat's back a few strokes. "Familiar is our secret weapon. I just wish I knew how to deploy him."

Nicole scooped Familiar into her lap and gave Jax another more lingering kiss on the cheek. "I wish I knew where Dad was being held. I've racked my brain, but I can't think of a single useful clue. So where are we going now?"

"We can deliver your attorney's laundry, but eventually we're going to have to end up at the Brown Derby to wait for Monica."

"That sounds dangerous," Nicole said, striving for a hint of humor. "She's going to be fit to be tied when she gets there and Richard Weeks doesn't show up.'' Jax had told her about the message he'd left on Monica's answering service.

''Yes, she'll be angry.'' Jax's grin said it all. Baiting Monica was fair sport after the way she'd behaved to everyone on the set.

''Why did you leave that message?'' Nicole asked. ''I mean how could you be sure she'd respond to her ex-husband's request?''

''I'm still not certain. But we needed to get her off the set tonight so that our absence would be less conspicuous. There was something in Richard Weeks's face when he spoke about Monica. I just had a gut feeling that she might risk John Hudson's ire for a chance to see Weeks again.''

''Do you think there are feelings still there?'' Nicole was surprised. ''It sounded as if the marriage between them contained a lot of unhappiness.''

''At one time, I'd be willing to bet there was a lot of love between them. At least from Richard's part.''

Nicole stared out the window, watching the scenery flash by. It was hard to imagine that Monica had ever been the kind of woman that could be truly loved. She was as prickly as a sand pear now. Maybe there was something to the curse.

''I suppose we should go to the Brown Derby and see what happens,'' Nicole said on a sigh. All she really wanted to do was figure out where her father was and to retrieve him.

''We have a bit of a wait. We could eat dinner,'' Jax suggested.

"Meow!" Familiar rose on his back legs and put a gentle paw on Jax's shoulder. "Meow."

"I think that's a vote for food," Jax said, laughing. "We've been neglecting Familiar's needs."

"After finding Dad gone, I never thought I'd be able to eat," Nicole said, "but I'm actually hungry, too."

"Then food it is," Jax said. "I happen to know a great place. Delicious seafood, outdoor tables," he eyed Nicole over Familiar's head, "and the best crème brûlée in the world."

FOOD HAS BEEN a neglected aspect of this case, for sure. I am famished. In fact, I'm so calorie challenged that I might swoon. Ah, for the days when women swooned. Talk about an art designed to make a man feel manly, that was the swoon. I somehow don't picture Nicole as the swooning type. She's more the kick-butt type. So when the chips are down would I rather have a swooner or a butt-kicker? That, my friends, isn't even a choice.

I am so hungry that I'm becoming delirious. At last we arrive at the restaurant. It's modest on the outside, but doing a great business. And there is the delicious odor of flame-licked goodies on a grill. Open the door, Nicole, and let me out! I'm ready to dine. And once the food is consumed, I have a better idea than going to the Brown Derby or the movie set. In my famished state, I haven't conveyed to my human partners the information I found in Richard's study. It isn't much, but they should know that Carlos

Sanchez handled the insurance claim. He was involved criminally and civilly. Of course the civil case came months after the criminal case. Still, it makes my whiskers twitch.

But all of that can hold long enough for a bite or two of dinner. This menu is extensive—ah, the blessing of choices. We've all indicated our choice of appetizers and I can hardly wait for the main course.

But my human counterparts have stopped reading and started staring into each other's eyes. Menu selection is out the window and romance is on the table. The way Jax is looking at Nicole makes me wonder if we'll be able to get through the meal. He's hungry, but it isn't food that he's interested in. Nor is she. They're just staring into each other's eyes, holding hands, touching. It's very sweet. But where are the appetizers?

I see the waiter headed our way. Yum, crab claws, for my initial foray into digestive bliss. Since Jax isn't going to let go of Nicole's hand long enough to eat, I'll sample his lobster bisque and the West Indies salad Nicole ordered. I think they had no intention of eating, but merely wanted to indulge me. Humans are trainable, they just take a lot of work.

I may have spoken too soon. Here comes a waiter with a very angry look on his face and he's staring right at me. You would think he'd never seen a cat dining at a table. I'd sit in a chair, but they aren't sized correctly for compact and elegant felines.

Oh, he's furious! The lout is claiming that cats are dirty and disease-ridden creatures and that I can't eat here. He's causing a scene about me! I never thought I'd live to see something like this. I've eaten in the finest establishments all over the world.

Jax and Nicole are holding him at bay. While they're arguing, I'm eating as fast as I can. I've finished the bisque and eaten at least half the crab claws. The guy is getting madder and madder. This is unreal.

For all of the famous California freewheeling life-styles, this guy is really uptight. Now Jax is getting annoyed. I can see it's going to be a standoff. Jax isn't going to yield and the waiter is going to get the manager. I supposed I'd better finish fast. I have a feeling we won't be here much longer.

But before we go I need to take a look at a phone book. If I can find what I'm looking for, it could save us a lot of time and energy.

While the food police try to argue with Jax and Nicole, I'll just slip on over to the little alcove where the hostess is hanging out. She's a pretty young woman with a big smile, and she's beckoning me over. I think she's getting a kick out of seeing the manager show his patoot.

WHEN JAX NOTICED that Familiar was missing, he felt a moment of panic. Then he saw the cat sashay over to the hostess station.

"You people simply must take your cat and leave," the manager said stiffly. "Now."

"I don't see a cat," Nicole pointed out with glee.

"You must have frightened him away. He's probably back in the kitchen by now."

Jax hid his grin. Nicole was about to give the poor man apoplexy. The idea of a cat in his kitchen was almost more than he could bear.

"I'll be back. We aren't finished here," the manager said as he hurried to make sure there were no felines in his cooking area.

"He's over by the hostess," Jax told Nicole as he rose from the table. "I'll grab him and we'll make a getaway. I think we've done enough damage here for the night."

"Not nearly enough," Nicole said. "That guy could have asked us nicely to leave with Familiar. He didn't have to come over and make a scene like that. It just backfired on him."

"Let me get Familiar," Jax said.

When he got inside, he wasn't the least surprised to find Familiar on top of the hostess's stand. The cat had pulled a telephone directory out and was turning the pages.

"Familiar!" Jax whispered to the cat. "You're in enough trouble here. I wouldn't compound things by asking to use a phone. I think I'll have to tell Eleanor and Peter to get you a cell phone."

The cat completely ignored him, and the young woman manning the hostess station gave Jax an amused look.

"He's a cat," she said. "He has no intention of obeying you."

"So I've noticed," Jax said.

He went to Familiar and tried to scoop him up, but the black cat evaded his efforts. Familiar went right back to the phone book. Jax bent down to examine what Familiar found so fascinating and discovered the cat was pouring over the insurance company ads in the yellow pages.

"We're going to need health insurance if you don't come with me," Jax whispered to him. "The manager has gone to check the kitchen for you. As soon as he realizes you're not there, he'll be coming back and we'll be history."

The hostess turned on a light, giving Familiar better illumination. "I don't see the harm in letting a cat eat at the table. You should see some of the children they allow to eat here. I'd imagine that a wild baboon would have better manners," she said. "As far as I could tell the cat was being perfectly behaved. Some folks are just way too uptight."

"I suspect it has something to do with health codes," Jax told her, watching as Familiar moved from one page to the other.

"Yeah, well, maybe the health codes need to be changed," the hostess said. "I've seen a lot of humans much nastier than a cat."

"Point well taken," Jax said. Out of the corner of his eye he saw the manager headed out to Nicole. She rose and began a charade of the helpless female. God, he loved her. She was the best. With Jax and the cat out of the way, Nicole had the manager eating out of her hand.

"Hurry, Familiar," Jax said. "Even the best actress can't hold up a show entirely by herself."

"Meow!" Familiar's black paw swatted at an ad—or at least the space between two ads.

Jax bent down to do a closer inspection. Familiar had pinpointed a space between Randall's Insurance Company and Rester's Full Service Insurance. Jax stared at the page, wondering what the cat was trying to tell him.

"Me-ow!" Familiar insistently swatted the space.

At last Jax understood. "Regency," he said. "The company that insured the diamond."

"That company's been closed for years," the hostess said. "I haven't thought about them in a long time."

"I understood they closed down," Jax said, immediately alert for anything he could learn. "Did you know the company?"

"Not really. I went to school with Allan Lancaster's daughter. It was a huge scandal, what with the theft of that big diamond. It was all in the tabloids about the curse and the tragic things that happened to anyone who touched the stone. And then Mr. Lancaster's insurance company went under. It was bad."

Jax stared at the girl. "You must have been about four at the time. How do you remember this?"

"I was eight," she said, whispering, "but don't tell my agent. He thinks I'm only twenty-two!"

Jax smiled. Everyone in Hollywood was either in the movie business or wanted to be. "Why do you remember this so clearly?"

"My mom wanted to be an actress before she got married and started a family. Monica Kane was her idol. We saw every film Ms. Kane ever did. Most of them we saw six or eight times. My mom could sew and she sometimes made clothes identical to the ones Ms. Kane wore in a movie or on a tour."

"Sounds like she was a big fan," Jax said.

"She really was. I remember the night of the Academy Awards. Mom was so certain Monica Kane would win. She'd invited all of her friends over for cocktails and to watch. When Monica didn't win, the whole party just went to pieces. Mama was devastated. That's when she told everyone about the curse of the diamond. I guess I remember because it scared the daylights out of me."

"I can imagine," Jax said. Out of the corner of his eye he saw that Familiar was still busy with the phone book. This time he was in the white pages.

"It was pretty traumatic for an eight-year-old. And I knew Misty Lancaster at school. Of course that's not her name now. She changed it when she started getting bigger parts in movies and things."

"Allan Lancaster's daughter became an actress?" Jax asked, immediately interested.

"Yeah. But I exaggerated some. I didn't really know Misty, I knew of her. Misty was always a little standoffish with me. My dad was a high school history teacher. Not very high up on the food chain of Los Angeles." She shook her head.

"It's a tough world."

"No kidding. But I'm up for a part in a terrific movie tomorrow. I'm going to kill 'em."

Jax grinned. "I'm sure you will."

"Meow!"

Familiar had finally found what he was looking for and he bent to examine the page. Allan Lancaster's name, number and address were right there.

"Good work, Familiar," Jax said, scratching the cat's head. "I think we have work to do."

"And just in time," the hostess said, nodding in the direction of the manager, the waiter and Nicole. The manager had finally seen the cat, perched on the hostess's desk. "Here comes trouble."

Jax slipped a twenty into the young woman's hand. "Good luck tomorrow," he said, picking up the cat. "I think we're about to be evicted."

"I'm sure you've been thrown out of better places than this," she said. "By the way, my name is Amanda Jones."

"Thanks, Amanda," Jax said, tucking Familiar under his arm and tracking right to avoid the scowling manager. He saw Nicole was monitoring his movements and plotting her course so they'd intersect at the parking lot.

"Let's get out of here," she said, picking up her pace when they were on the gravel of the lot.

"I didn't pay for the food," Jax said, ready to hand Familiar off to Nicole.

"Don't worry, the manager said since we were leaving, we didn't have to pay."

"Hey, we could use Familiar to get free meals all over town."

At Familiar's hiss of resentment, Jax and Nicole both laughed.

"I have another lead," Jax said as he got in the truck and put Familiar on the seat between them. "I don't believe in coincidence, but that young woman at the hostess counter gave me the name of the man who owned Regency Insurance."

"The company that held the policy on the Dream of Isis," Nicole said. "That's a perfect lead to follow."

"Yes, Allan Lancaster may know something that can really help us, if he'll talk to us," Jax said.

"If he'll talk," Nicole agreed.

Jax drove out of the parking lot and in a moment they were in the frantic traffic, headed for another part of the city.

Chapter Fifteen

Nicole and Jax stood in the neat entranceway of Allan Lancaster's home and rang the doorbell. They'd been tempted to call but felt a sudden appearance might yield more information, or at least give them a chance to watch Allan Lancaster's expression.

Nicole saw Familiar slip around the hedges of the house and she was about to call him back when she heard the sound of a lock being turned from inside the house.

The front door opened and the middle-aged man who stood there started to speak. He took one look at Nicole, though, and stepped back. Sweat popped up on his forehead.

Nicole watched in astonishment and then concern as Allan Lancaster tried to say something. No sound came from him.

"Mr. Lancaster?" Nicole started forward to grab his arm. She thought Allan Lancaster was having a heart attack.

Lancaster put his hand to his heart and stumbled backward, crying out something unintelligible.

"Mr. Lancaster," Jax said, rushing forward and supporting the man. "Are you hurt?"

Allan Lancaster shook his head, taking a few moments to catch his breath before he tried to say anything. "No, I'm fine. It's her." He pointed at Nicole.

Nicole stood in the doorway, absolutely frozen. She had no idea what Allan Lancaster was talking about.

Jax supported the man for a few seconds more, until he was steady enough to stand on his own. "Why did Nicole startle you?" Jax asked.

"She looks like…" Allan Lancaster clamped his lips shut. "She looks like someone I know," he said. "I didn't expect to see her here."

"Who would that be?" Jax pressed.

"It doesn't matter. What do you want?"

Nicole realized that Allan had recovered his equilibrium. Though they'd had the advantage of surprise, he was quickly regaining his balance.

"We'd like to talk to you about your insurance company," Jax said.

"I don't have an insurance company," Allan said bitterly. "I once had a company, but it was stolen from me by a thief."

Nicole started to rebut Allan's statement, but she checked herself. She focused instead on his reaction to her when he first saw her. It was extreme. And now he was reluctant to reveal who he thought she looked like.

On the ride Jax had told her all about Amanda Jones and the conversation they'd shared at the hostess's desk. She suddenly put it together. Stepping forward, she caught his full attention. "Your daughter is Angela Myers, isn't she?" Nicole asked.

Nicole saw that her guess had struck home. Allan Lancaster blanched.

"Please leave," Allan said. He didn't answer Nicole's question, but he didn't have to. The truth was evident.

Nicole took a deep breath. Now it all made sense. No wonder Angela was so mean to her. Angela knew who she was, knew her past history—and hated her for it. The stolen earring and Monica's broach had been a deliberate setup. Angela had attempted to make Nicole pay for the past.

"Is Angela your daughter?" Jax asked.

"Yes," Allan said, smiling a bitter smile. "Do you know Angela? It broke her mother's heart when she changed her name for the movies. She was born Misty Lancaster, but Angela thought Misty was a name that dated her. She didn't want to be thought of as a child of the flower generation."

"Have you seen Angela lately?" Nicole asked. There was something in the way Allan spoke of his daughter that hinted at a breach between them. And why would a father be so shocked to see his daughter? Allan Lancaster had almost suffered a physical illness at the sight of her.

"No, I haven't seen Angela," Allan said. "Is she in some kind of trouble?"

"No," Nicole reassured him. "I'm working with her on a movie set."

"Yes, she's become quite successful. I read about her all the time."

There it was again, that hint of estrangement.

"Why are you here?" Allan asked, suddenly suspicious again. "If you work with Angela you see her every day. Why are you here? You said she wasn't in trouble. What's wrong? Who are you?"

Nicole had never suspected that Angela Myers had parents. In truth, if Nicole had been asked, she would have said that Angela was cloned and raised by aliens. Allan Lancaster was a man embittered by the twists of fate his life had taken, and it was clear he blamed Vincent Paul for the ruination of his business, but Allan seemed to dote on his daughter. So what had happened to turn Angela into such a witch?

Nicole caught the look of eagerness that passed over Jax's face and decided to let him handle it.

"Nothing is actually wrong, Mr. Lancaster. But we do need to talk with you."

"About what?"

"It's about the Dream of Isis."

"Get away from my house!" Allan Lancaster said each word distinctly and with emphasis. "Get out now before I call the police."

Allan's reaction was so strong that Nicole stepped forward, concerned that he might have another attack of illness.

"Please, Mr. Lancaster. We don't mean to upset you but we need your help."

"Who are you?" he demanded.

"I'm Nicole Paul and this is Jax McClure."

"Paul," Allan said through gritted teeth. "Your Vincent Paul's daughter, aren't you?"

"I am," Nicole said, "and my father is in serious trouble because of the Dream of Isis."

"I won't have that stone mentioned in my home! It ruined me. I don't know what kind of people you are, but I want you off my property now."

"Mr. Lancaster, please," Nicole intervened. "My father's life is in danger."

"I don't allow the name of that stone to be spoken in my home," Lancaster said angrily. "The day I closed my insurance company was the last time I had to talk about that cursed stone. I never owned it. I only held it once, and look what it did to me."

"Do you really believe the stone is cursed?" Jax asked, his voice neutral.

"I most certainly do. You can't begin to imagine what happened to me. I had a thriving business. I was selling policies to some of the biggest names in Hollywood. I was on the verge of getting involved with underwriting the accident policies for some of the movies. It was all just about to happen for me, and then Richard Weeks asked me to insure that blasted diamond because some actress was going to wear it on the night of the Oscars."

"It was a short-term policy?" Jax asked, diverting Allan's attention for the moment.

"Only for ninety days. That was the length of time Vincent Paul, blast his rotted soul, was going to have the diamond in his possession."

Nicole felt as if she'd been punched in the stomach. The way Allan cursed her father's name made her physically ill. But she forced her shoulders back and stepped forward slightly. "Vincent Paul is innocent," she said softly. "He never stole that stone and he spent twenty years in prison for something he didn't do."

Allan's face suffused with blood but his pale eyes still held an angry glint of fire. "I'm sorry for you. You were just a child. I remember seeing you at the jewelry store several times. You were an innocent victim, but I won't take back what I said. Vincent Paul ruined me. He stole that diamond and I had to pay out on the policy. It destroyed my business and my life."

"My father didn't steal anything," Nicole said, clenching her teeth to keep from letting loose a torrent of angry comments. "He spent his best years in prison for a crime he didn't commit."

"He went to prison for stealing that diamond. Twenty years is what he got, and now that he's out of jail his time is up. I didn't do anything wrong, and I'm still serving time. My wife left me. My daughter started to look at me like I was a bumbling incompetent. No other insurance company would hire me. They thought I was jinxed!"

"I'm sorry for what happened to you," Nicole said, though she was finding it hard to muster any real sympathy for Allan. He was too quick to blame everything on someone else. He seemed to have forgotten that he wrote a policy on a valuable stone. He made that decision and no one else.

"I don't need pity," Allan said. He looked down at the floor. "In fact, I don't know what I need."

"My father didn't steal the...that diamond," Nicole said in a forceful voice.

"Then who did?" Allan asked. "Just tell me who else had the code to his safe? Who could have opened the safe, scooped up the diamond and walked out like that?"

"I don't know," Nicole said, "but that's exactly what I intend to find out."

"You don't have to look far. Your father took that diamond. I went to his store. I checked out his security system. It was one of the most advanced for that time. I'd never have insured the diamond otherwise."

"Were you aware that Monica Kane knew the combination to that safe?" Jax asked.

Allan turned his full attention from Nicole and to Jax. "What are you saying?" he asked.

"I'm not saying anything. I'm pointing out a fact. Monica Kane knew the combination to the safe. She could have opened it at any time."

"I thought Vincent was smarter than that," Allan said on a whisper. "He swore to me that no one knew the combination but himself. He promised me he'd never tell a soul. Damn him for a fool. Are you sure he told Monica?"

"Monica told me herself," Jax said.

"Why would Vincent do such a thing?" Allan asked, and for the first time there was a hint of doubt in his voice. "Before I insured that stone, I talked to him about security. He promised that no one could open that safe except him.''

''I think Monica needed some assurance that she could get the stone if something happened to Vincent,'' Jax said. ''She can be a very persuasive woman.''

''Indeed,'' Allan said. ''I knew better than to get involved with the Dream of Isis. I saw it once, and I was dazzled by the stone, and by Ms. Kane. I lost my judgment and it cost me everything, including my daughter.''

''Angela is perfectly fine,'' Jax assured him.

''Yes, she's physically fine. A lovely young woman. But she despises me. She thinks I'm weak and foolish. She blames me because we lost everything and then her mother left me. Left us both.'' He shrugged. ''It was very hard on her. It made her bitter.''

Nicole could certainly have agreed with that assessment of Angela, but she wisely kept her mouth shut. There was no point in rubbing salt in Allan's wounds.

''Mr. Lancaster, I don't want to involve you in the details of what's going on, but Mr. Paul's life may be in danger. He's been kidnapped.'' Jax paused.

Nicole watched Allan's face as he digested the possible meanings of what Jax said.

''Then if someone has taken Vincent, either he does have the diamond and they want it back, or he doesn't have it and they think he does.''

''It's the latter,'' Nicole said stoutly. ''My father

would never have stolen, and he would never have ruined the lives of so many people. Trust me, if he had any idea where the diamond is, he would have told me. But I do know if we don't find him, there's a chance he may die. He has a heart condition.''

Allan Lancaster considered for a long moment. ''I don't think there's anything I can do to help you, but I'll try. Come on in.''

Nicole was just stepping over the threshold when Familiar darted in front of her. In a flash the cat had scampered down the dark hall and into the interior of the house. Allan Lancaster never noticed him.

Jax gave a brief shrug at Nicole's questioning look and they followed Allan into a den.

''What is it you want?'' Allan asked.

''How did you come to insure that diamond?'' Nicole asked.

''That's a good question. I was an independent office for Regency, which was small potatoes compared to the other giant insurance companies. You always hear about Lloyd's of London and that type of agency when it comes to such high-profile jewels as the Dream…as that diamond,'' Allan said.

''So how did you happen to insure it?'' Jax said, bringing Allan back to the question.

''I was trying my darndest to break into the movie business, and by that I mean writing insurance policies for productions. There are thousands of areas of liability on a movie set. What I was most interested in was physical liability. Sort of writing the accident coverage for the production side.''

Nicole knew a little about such policies since she was covered as a stuntwoman. She nodded.

"Mist— I mean Angela had expressed an interest in being an actress at a very young age. I knew that if I had some connections in the business, even via insurance, I might be able to make some contacts for her."

For the first time since meeting him, Nicole felt a real pang of sympathy for Allan. He truly loved his daughter and he'd planned his career around helping her. As far as she could tell, Angela didn't appreciate a bit of it.

"But who brought you the diamond to insure?" Jax asked, once again pulling the conversation back on track.

"Technically, it was a Realtor, Richard Weeks. He owned the diamond, but it was the insurance company's lawyer who set it all up. He said he knew a client who had a valuable stone that needed a short-term insurance policy."

"Who was that lawyer?" Nicole asked. Her gut was knotting in anticipation of the answer.

"Arnold Anderson," Allan said. When he saw the look on Nicole's face, he continued. "Do you know him?"

"Indeed," Nicole said. "He went to work for Carlos Sanchez, the lawyer who represented my father in the criminal case. Didn't you know that?"

Allan frowned. "No, I never put it together."

"Wouldn't that be a conflict of interest?" Nicole asked.

"It's looking like a little more than that," Jax said. "Mr. Lancaster, have you had any dealings with Sanchez since then?"

"I don't see where that's really pertinent to any of this," Allan said, once again bristling.

"It may have a lot to do with it," Nicole said. She leaned forward. "Mr. Lancaster, I love my father. If you know anything that might help us, please tell us."

Allan hesitated. "Mis— Angela got into some trouble about five months ago. Legal trouble. Carlos Sanchez has a big name around here. I hired him and he helped her out."

"Very big of him," Nicole said bitterly. "I hate to ask, but what kind of trouble was Angela in?"

"Bad debt," he said. "She has to look good to get jobs, and those clothes are very expensive. She has to have a nice address or casting agents won't think she's successful. She says that's the kiss of death. She has to project the illusion of success even when times are lean."

"Thank you," Nicole said. She looked over at Jax to see if he was ready. She'd gotten plenty of information and she knew right where she wanted to go. Carlos Sanchez was not going to be happy to see her.

"One more thing," Jax said as he rose to his feet. "When we find the diamond, we're going to prove Vincent innocent of all charges, and then we'll return the diamond to you. Your company paid out for the value of the diamond. You can sell it or do whatever you please with it."

"I'm not certain I want it," Allan said. "I do believe it's cursed. I highly advise both of you not to touch it or look upon it. I lost everything I ever dreamed of having because of that stone. Maybe it should simply be returned to Egypt and sent back to the tomb it was taken from.''

"Perhaps that's what should be done," Nicole agreed. "But you'll be the person who makes that choice.''

Allan showed them to the door. Nicole felt a sense of sadness as she stepped from the entranceway to the sidewalk. Familiar, quicker than a flash of lightning, darted out of the door just before it closed. Nicole bent down and scooped the cat up in her arms, then turned and looked back at the house.

"Find anything, buddy?" she asked the cat.

He gazed into her eyes and blinked twice.

"I take that as a no," she said, kissing the top of his head. "He's just a sad man whose life has been ruined just like my father. Whatever happened with that diamond, a lot of good people were hurt.''

"I'm not a believer in curses and superstitions," Jax said as he opened the truck door for her, "but I don't want that diamond in my possession. I think when we find it, we'll just call the authorities and let them deal with it.''

"I know what you mean," Nicole said, putting Familiar on the front seat as she climbed in the truck. "Either that, or I may implant it in one very slick lawyer.''

"Carlos Sanchez," Jax said as he got in on the driver's side and started the truck. "Our next destination.''

Chapter Sixteen

Jax had just pulled out into the flow of traffic when his cell phone rang. He answered, and then removed the phone from his ear as John Hudson's voice barked at him.

"Where are you?" John demanded.

Jax returned the phone to his ear. "Something came up," he said, knowing those were words that could get him fired.

"What do you mean 'something came up'? You're due on the set. We've been waiting for you. We're held up with a full crew ready to film. Where in the hell are you?" John asked again. "And you'd better be on your way to the set. We have everything ready for this sequence except you and Nicole. I assume the two of you are together."

"We are," Jax said. "John, something important came up. I don't want to go into it over the phone, but I'll tell you about it tomorrow. You just have to believe me that it was important enough that I let you down and risked ruining my name in the business."

"I don't want excuses, I want you here."

"Is Monica ready?" Jax asked, hoping that once John realized his star wasn't on the set he'd shift his ire to a new target.

"Monica?" John hesitated. "She's in her trailer, waiting for you to show up."

"She told me she had something she had to do tonight," Jax began before John interrupted him.

"Monica is a professional. She wouldn't dare—" He broke off. "Timmy, go to Ms. Kane's trailer and make sure she's getting ready for this scene. I'm back, Jax, and I'm angry. I hope you have a good explanation for this and I'm ready to hear it now."

Jax held the phone against his ear for a moment. "I can't tell you now, John. But I will tell you. Everything. Just know that this is very important or I'd never let you down."

"Hold on a minute, Jax." There was the sound of John talking with someone. His voice grew more agitated. "I'm back," he said to Jax. "When will you be here? Is Monica with you? Has something happened to her?"

"Monica isn't with me. I'll be in touch," Jax said. He realized that no matter how much time had passed, John still loved Monica Kane. He slowly pressed the end button and lowered the phone.

"He sent Timmy to check Monica's trailer," he said. "He realizes that she isn't on the set, and I think he's more concerned about her now than the fact that we aren't there."

"If he puts two and two together he'll suspect we

had something to do with Monica's disappearance from the set," Nicole said.

"He may," Jax said, accepting the consequences of his actions. "There's nothing we can do about that right now. Once he discovers she's gone to meet Richard…" He didn't finish the thought. "I find it both sad and inspiring that he continues to love her after all these years."

"*Sad* is the word I'd choose. As Richard Weeks pointed out, Monica changed. She isn't the woman John fell in love with."

"Only he can figure that out for himself," Jax said.

"You're just a romantic at heart," Nicole teased him. "Undying love appeals to you."

Jax drove for a few seconds. "I guess it does. I've never been the kind of man who enjoyed temporary relationships."

Normally Jax never talked about his feelings, but he found that it was important to make sure Nicole understood how deeply he'd begun to care for her.

"I was involved with a woman back in Texas. We were high school sweethearts and I thought we had the best of all futures—ranching and raising our kids."

There was a long pause and he felt Nicole take his hand and hold it. His fingers curled around hers and he was once again surprised by her strength and her ability to comfort him with just a touch.

"What happened?" she asked.

"A pretty common story. My girl wanted to get

her college degree. I'd already gone deep into debt on the ranch. She went off to college and decided there was more to the world than a Texas cattle farm. It almost killed me. I lost her and the farm.''

"That must have been hard,'' Nicole said.

"I didn't have a diamond to blame it on, but I sure lost my dream,'' he said. "But I survived and I moved out to Los Angeles to do stunts. I used to do some rodeoing and I met a guy at Amarillo who suggested I give the movies a try. So here I am.''

"And your girl?''

"She's a bank manager in Dallas. She married a lawyer and has two kids. She's happy.'' He pulled Nicole closer to him. "And so am I. You know, I didn't realize it until I started thinking about it, but I am happy. Since you came into my life, a lot of doors that I'd closed and locked have begun to come open. I see a future for us, Nicole. Together.''

"I'm beginning to believe in a lot of things I never thought I'd allow myself to believe in,'' Nicole said. "Things like trust and loyalty and love. And permanence. You've given me those things, Jax.''

"My folks have been married for forty years,'' Jax said. "That's sort of what I was taught to expect— a real partnership. If one of my parents were to die, I think the other one would follow shortly after.''

"My parents loved each other very much, too,'' Nicole said. "If it wasn't for me, my father probably would have quit living, too. Sometimes I forget how much my father has lost in his life.''

"Your dad was lucky,'' Jax said. "He had you to

focus his love on. I'm sure that's what kept him going in prison. And what's keeping him going now."

"Jax, do you think he's still alive?"

He heard the fear in her voice and he reached across the truck to touch her.

Familiar hopped over her lap and got near the door. Then, with an adamant growl, he began butting her with his head.

"What?" Nicole asked, tears still in her voice as she wiped at her cheeks. "What is it you want, you crazy cat?"

"I think he wants you to scoot over," Jax said. "I know I do."

Nicole moved across the bench seat until she was sitting close to Jax. It was the most natural thing in the world for him to slip his arm around her shoulders and pull her tightly against his side.

"This is standard practice in Texas," he said. "If a guy has a girl and a pickup, then the girl rides by his side."

"I think I might like Texas," Nicole admitted. She snuggled a little closer to him.

Jax sometimes had to remind himself how vulnerable Nicole was. She was tough and strong physically, but she was very fragile emotionally. He let his hand wander over her shoulder and arm, caressing and comforting.

"Your dad's going to be fine," he reassured her. "We're going to find him and we're going to find that cursed diamond. This nightmare is going to end for everyone."

"Take a left here," Nicole said. "I think at this time of night Carlos Sanchez will be at his home rather than his office."

"I've been trying to think of how we should approach this," Jax said. "Do you have any ideas?"

"I know how I'd like to do it—tie him in a chair and make him tell me the truth. But I guess that's only an option in a movie."

"I think torture is definitely out," Jax said, hugging her a little closer. "So what's next?"

"I'm still trying to put all of it together," Nicole said. "What would it benefit Carlos to do all of this, if he is behind it? He ruined Allan Lancaster and my father, and yet he doesn't have the diamond."

"That's a good point," Jax said. "Whoever has your father doesn't have the diamond. They still want the Dream of Isis."

"We really aren't any closer to solving this than we were two days ago," Nicole said with a tone of desperation, "and I fear my father's time is running out. Once they realize he really doesn't know where the diamond is, they'll kill him."

Jax didn't respond to that and she knew he'd already thought about it. Her father's usefulness was limited.

"We have direct ties to Carlos Sanchez and Richard Weeks," Jax said, going over what they'd learned. "We have Allan Lancaster, too. We have Monica Kane, and in a limited sort of way Angela Meyers."

"Any of them could be the thief," Nicole said,

"but I find it hard to believe that Monica could have been behind all of this."

"She's the most logical choice," Jax pointed out.

"I know. It's just hard to believe that Monica engineered all of this to steal a jewel she can never display in public. And if what we've heard so far is true, Monica blames the curse of the diamond for short-circuiting her acting career. She doesn't really want it."

Jax didn't disagree with Nicole's reasoning. In fact, he was right with her. But who did have the diamond? And why had they taken it?

"I suppose we can rule Allan Lancaster and Angela out as the thieves," Jax said. "Their lives were drastically altered and not for the better."

"The same could be said for my father, but no one seems to take that into consideration," Nicole said. "But I believe you're right. Angela is awful. I think she planted her earring and Monica's broach on me to try and frame me just as an attempt to get even with my father."

"She wanted to hurt you for something that happened twenty years ago, when you were a child," Jax said. "She's a terrible person, but I think if she had access to the Dream of Isis she'd be living high on the hog, not having to hire lawyers to get her out of financial difficulties."

"Your point is taken," Nicole said.

"So that leaves Sanchez and Weeks." Jax followed the directions Nicole gave him as he talked.

''Do you think Weeks was telling us the truth?''
Nicole asked.

Jax heard the doubt in her voice. He understood
more fully now why Nicole found it so difficult to
trust people. All of her life she'd been tricked. Starting with the charge against her father, Nicole had
lived in a world where the facts she knew ran counter
to what everyone else said. It wasn't a world where
trust was easily built.

''I did believe him,'' Jax said. ''I think he truly
loved Monica and that he was devastated when she
changed.''

''So we're stuck with Carlos Sanchez.'' Nicole
glanced back at the suit that was hanging in the plastic dry cleaner's bag. ''Do you think he's dangerous?''

Jax didn't have an answer. ''I think we need to be
very careful.''

''My father might be at his house,'' Nicole said,
excitement creeping into her voice.

''Don't get your hopes up, Nicole. If Sanchez has
your father, I doubt he would be holding him at his
home.''

In the lights of the dash he saw the hope slip from
her face and he knew the crush of disappointment,
too. He hated hurting Nicole, even in the smallest
way. But worse than telling her the truth now would
be seeing her devastated later on.

''You're right,'' she said softly. ''I just want to
find Dad and make sure he's okay.''

"Nicole, what do you think about calling the police?" Jax asked.

"No! They said not to call the police. I'm afraid they'll hurt Dad if we call the cops."

Jax nodded. "Okay," he said. "But I have to take into account your safety. If Carlos Sanchez is behind all of this, he may be a very dangerous man. If he feels trapped, he could do anything. We might need backup."

"Meow!"

Up until that time Familiar had been very quiet. He slipped into Nicole's lap and began patting the cell phone Jax had in his pocket.

"He wants you to call someone," Nicole said. "Not the cops!"

"No, but he has a plan," Jax said, pulling out the phone and holding it in his palm. "When I said backup, that's when he got excited."

"Is there anyone you trust?" Nicole asked.

"That's an interesting question," Jax said. "I always thought I trusted most people, but when your safety is at stake, I'm not sure I trust anyone at all."

"I can call Connie," Nicole said, her eyes opening. "I trust her."

"She could help," Jax said, discovering that though he hardly knew the teenager, he trusted her also. "Give her a call."

Nicole took the phone and dialed her number. In a couple of rings, Connie breathlessly answered.

"Where in the hell are you?" she asked, adding, "Excuse my French, but I'm worried to death about you. Everyone on the set is going crazy looking for you and Jax and Monica Kane. Mr. Hudson's talking about calling the police on the two of you. He thinks you've abducted Monica.''

"We don't have Monica," Nicole said, "but we are in a pinch. Connie, I need your help."

"Well, sure, just tell me what to do," Connie said.

"It could jeopardize your part in the movie."

"The way I look at that is that I wouldn't have had a chance to be in the movie if it wasn't for you. You took a big risk helping me. And you didn't act like it was a big deal at all. The movie is great, but your friendship is the important thing. Just tell me what you need me to do. And I should mention that Jason is right here with me, and he's signaling that he wants to help, too."

Nicole relayed the information to Jax and then handed him the phone.

"Connie, you need to write this information down. Nicole and I are going to see a man named Carlos Sanchez." He gave her Carlos's address and phone number. "If we don't call you back in thirty minutes, send the cops to that address, okay? The only other thing we have is a phone number that Familiar found. We haven't been able to track it down, but it could be a lead." He gave her the number from the slip of paper Familiar had found in the drugstore parking lot.

"I've got it," Connie said. "You know, as much as I dislike the cops, I think it's time you called them. This could get really serious."

He felt Nicole's fingers dig into his arm. He looked at her and shook his head. "It's okay. We have to do this our way."

"I still don't like it, but I'll do what you ask," Connie said.

Jax could hear Connie repeating everything to Jason.

"And there's one other thing, Connie," Jax said. "Make sure Monica isn't in her trailer, and then I need you to sneak in and search it."

"Search Ms. Kane's trailer?" Connie asked, her voice rising. "If I get caught I'll be sent back to jail. What am I looking for?"

Jax only wished he could tell her specifically. "Look through any papers and see if you can find Carlos Sanchez's name. And check her jewelry. See if there's a lavender diamond. A huge stone."

"She wouldn't leave valuable diamonds in her trailer," Connie said. "She isn't stupid."

"No, but it's worth at least looking."

"Okay, Jax, I'll do it for Nicole. Jason wants to talk to you."

In a second Jax heard his roommate's voice on the phone.

"Jax, do you want me to meet you at that address? I can be very helpful."

Jax considered it. "Are you sure, Jason? You might be biting off a world of trouble."

"Hey, man, I'm not about to let you go down alone. I'll be there. It's not that far from the set."

"Thanks," Jax said, feeling more than a little relieved to know that he would have backup. With Jason's skills they might be able to plan a sneak attack rather than a frontal assault.

I DON'T KNOW what's going through Jax's mind, but I can see that he's thinking hard. I'm a bit surprised that Jason was with Connie. He struck me as the kind of guy who liked his women dark and sophisticated. And I thought he had a girlfriend. Marla something. But maybe his interest in Connie is just friendly. I'll have to keep an eye on that and make sure my little Arkansas flower doesn't get hurt.

But we have bigger fish to fry right now. Carlos Sanchez. His name keeps popping up in this case. I find it more than a little suspicious that he'd volunteer to defend Nicole for free. That should have been the first tip-off. But what does he want? The diamond? That's the troubling thing. I would have thought he had the diamond. All of our primary suspects in this case want the diamond. None of them seem to have it. We need to figure out where that stone is!

There's something that doesn't add up here. I just hope that we can figure it out and find Nicole's father before something tragic happens.

It was a good idea to search Monica's trailer. I wish I was there to help Connie. She could use a little expertise from a black kitty. But I also need to be here to help Nicole and Jax. That's the problem with being indispensable—everyone needs me.

We're closing in on Carlos. Nicole says he lives

on this road. And there's Jason on the motorcycle. That's good, all of our forces are here together.

Wow! Carlos doesn't have a house, he has a castle. Plenty of space in there for a dungeon. Maybe Vincent is here after all.

Well, I suppose there's nothing to do now but go in, guns blasting. It's show time!

Chapter Seventeen

Nicole knocked on the door of Carlos Sanchez's home. She was still a little surprised that the powerful lawyer didn't have some kind of security force, but it worked in her favor. In the plan that she and Jax and Familiar had hurriedly thrown together, she was going to pretend she was so distraught over her father's abduction that she had come to Carlos for help.

While she was busy crying on Carlos's shoulder, Jax, Jason and Familiar would find a way to enter the house and search it. The three of them could cover the house fairly quickly, making sure that Vincent wasn't being held somewhere.

The front door opened and Nicole was further surprised when Carlos stood in front of her. She'd expected a butler or some minion.

"Nicole," Carlos said, frowning, "what are you doing here?"

"Dad's been abducted," she said, and her tears weren't pretend. She was worried sick about her father. She began to cry in earnest as Carlos put an arm around her and gently led her into the house.

"Are you sure about all of this?" Carlos asked as he settled her in a huge leather chair.

"There was a ransom note of sorts. It's all about that damn diamond," Nicole said. "They want the diamond and they're trying to force Daddy to tell them where it is."

"The Dream of Isis," Carlos said, shaking his head. "How many lives has that stone ruined?"

"You have to help me," Nicole pleaded. "I don't know what to do. I'm afraid to go to the cops. They said they'd hurt Dad if I did. What should I do, Carlos?"

He patted her shoulder paternally. "We'll think of something, Nicole. Of course, the easiest thing would be for your father to give up the diamond."

"Give up the diamond?" Nicole frowned, wiping at her eyes with a tissue he gave her. "What do you mean?"

"Vincent is a grand performer, but everyone knows he stole that diamond and hid it. Now that he's out of prison, he's going to recover it and sell it for a fortune. He'll end up being well paid for the twenty years he spent in jail. Your father is not a stupid man." Carlos laughed softly. "No, he's a very smart man. He managed to keep that diamond under wraps for two decades. Everyone who knew anything about the case has been relentlessly hunting the Dream of Isis. No one has even come close to finding it."

"But what if Daddy doesn't have the diamond?" Nicole asked, all wide-eyed innocence. "He said he didn't take it. You know that. You defended him in the trial."

"Of course I defended him, but I knew he had the stone."

"Daddy told you he had it?"

"Your father is far too clever for that. He always insisted he was innocent. No matter how I tried to convince him to give up the diamond, he always said he didn't have it. Yes, Vincent is a very clever man. He's followed his plan with great dedication. I admire that."

Nicole saw it all then. The man who'd been hired to help her father had never really tried. He'd taken the money—Vincent's life savings and the cash from the sale of the jewelry shop—and he'd never made a real effort to prove her father innocent. All along his only interest had been in worming the location of the diamond from Vincent. Anger shot through her, and she fought to control her expression. She couldn't afford to let Carlos see what she was thinking.

"Where do you think Vincent hid the diamond?" Carlos asked as he poured Nicole a glass of brandy and handed it to her.

"I don't believe my father took the stone," she said, struggling to control her emotions. She wanted to hurt Carlos like he'd hurt her and her family. He'd betrayed them.

Because he believed Vincent had the diamond all along.

A cold chill ran over Nicole as the implications of this scattered through her mind. Carlos had her father. She knew it in her heart. And he would kill Vincent, and her, if the slightest problem arose.

"If your father had simply told me where the diamond was, I could have gotten his sentence reduced or an early parole. But he was a stubborn man. He wanted the stone for himself."

"Carlos, you're wrong. You've been wrong the whole time. Dad doesn't have the diamond," she said. She tried to keep her voice soft, to play along in the role of worried daughter seeking advice, but she was finding it increasingly difficult to do so. Carlos was beginning to scare her. He'd become obsessed by the Dream of Isis. His greed for the stone had touched every aspect of his life.

"Nicole, you are so naive," Carlos said. "It's part of your charm. Your undying loyalty to Vincent is priceless. But enough time has passed. The fact that you came here tonight, alone, gives me an interesting opportunity. Would you like to know what it is?"

"I don't know," Nicole said, and her confusion wasn't part of her dramatic role. "What are you talking about?" The word *opportunity* on Carlos's lips didn't sound very healthy.

"Vincent has been reluctant to help me," Carlos said. He shrugged his shoulders as if it were a negligible thing. "Like you, he insists he doesn't have the stone. But I believe that if he thinks I'm going to hurt you, he'll tell me. You are the lever that's going to roll over the stone concealing the Dream of Isis,'' Carlos said. ''You walked in here as if it was your destiny.''

JAX HAD TAKEN the third floor of the huge house while Jason was searching the second floor. Familiar, because he was like a quick shadow moving through the rooms, was on the first floor.

Jax would have preferred to be on the first floor with Nicole, so he could keep an eye on what was happening. But he could serve better where he was.

He moved through the rooms using a small, intense flashlight he'd taken from the truck. So far he'd found only a lot of expensive furnishings.

He checked his watch again. Ten minutes had elapsed. He'd found nothing, and there wasn't a sign of a living soul on the third floor. It looked as if the suites of bedrooms were never used.

Caution and speed were constant elements of his job. Timing was the third. All good stuntpeople needed those things to remain safe and pull off the job. He'd always excelled in those areas, as did Nicole. No matter how ineffective he felt at the moment, he had to keep looking and he had to trust that Nicole could handle herself. He opened another door and swung the light through the darkness.

Nothing.

He stepped back into the hall and froze. He didn't need to see the weapon to identify the gun barrel that was poking in his spine.

"Mr. Sanchez would like a word with you."

Jax slowly turned around in disbelief. "Jason?" he said. "What are you doing?"

"My job," Jason said with a tight smile. "Making sure that you don't spoil everything. Mr. Sanchez is so very happy that Nicole stopped in for a chat. She's going to be the grease that lubricates Vincent's tongue. He's an ornery old coot."

Jax had recovered from the shock of Jason's betrayal, but he was still digesting what had occurred. "You've been working for Sanchez all along."

"You've got it," Jason said, pushing Jax toward the staircase. "He had it all planned out. He knew to the moment when Vincent would get out of jail, and he knew that the old man's only weakness was his daughter."

"All for that diamond?" Jax said almost under his breath. "Is Vincent here?"

"First floor," Jason said, motioning Jax to descend the stairs. "You'll see him soon enough."

"Is he okay?"

"He claims he has a heart condition, and we did get his medication for him. He seems fine to me," Jason said. "Of course that might not last much longer if he doesn't tell us where that diamond is hidden. Mr. Sanchez is a patient man, but after twenty years, he's becoming a little unhappy."

Jax moved slowly along the staircase, his mind rushing from one possible action to another. He had to do something. "You've bet on the wrong horse,"

Jax said, keeping his voice strong and level. "Vincent doesn't have the diamond. He never did."

"Oh, right," Jason said. "That's a great story, but we know the truth. He's got it and he's going to give it up, one way or the other."

"Where's Nicole?" Jax asked.

"With her father." Jason laughed softly. "I'm sure they're delighted to see each other."

"If you hurt her—"

"What will you do, cowboy?" Jason said, jamming the gun harder into Jax's back.

"Why are you doing this?"

"Money. Sanchez pays quite well. Now quit talking and walk. We need to get this over with and find that diamond. This has gone on way too long. I've got a home waiting for me in South America. Fantastic place, and it'll be all paid for once Mr. Sanchez gets that diamond."

"You know you're going to get caught," Jax said.

"If you're counting on Connie, I wouldn't. She's a little tied up at the moment."

Jax felt his hopes tumble. He had been counting on Connie. She was just a kid, but she was a smart one. "You didn't hurt her, did you?"

"Just a little sedative to make sure she stays conked out. She'll be fine. Let me give you a tip. If I were you, I'd be a little worried about my hide, Jax. You're the expendable one in the group."

NICOLE STEPPED through the open door and into the dimness of the room. The heavy oak door slammed behind her, and she heard the lock slide into place. Stepping forward gingerly, she made out the form of a man stretched out on a bed. "Dad?" she called as she ran forward.

Vincent Paul instantly sat up. "Nicole, how did he get you? I tried to warn you—"

"I'm fine. I'm just so glad to see you. Are you okay?"

Vincent grasped her hands. "This isn't about me. I don't matter. What matters is that you're safe."

"Dad, Carlos is behind all of this. He thinks you have the diamond."

"I know," Vincent said tiredly. "I'm beginning to wish that I did have it. I'd give it to him. I tell him I don't know where it is and he laughs at me. He thinks I want the diamond so badly that I'll risk you."

"All along he set us up," Nicole said. She was getting angrier and angrier. Twenty years of Vincent's life was gone. She'd missed having a father her entire teenage and young adult years. Her life had been ruined by a man who refused to take no for an answer.

"What are we going to do?" Vincent asked. "When he finds out I don't have the stone, I'm afraid he's going to hurt you."

"Don't give up yet," Nicole said. Jax and Jason were somewhere in the house, along with Familiar. They weren't defeated yet.

"Can you walk?" Nicole asked her father.

"As in getting out of here?" Vincent asked. "Of course. They haven't harmed me."

"Get ready," she said, whispering. She leaned closer to his ear. "The cavalry is about ready to ride over the hill."

Just as she finished speaking, the door of the room opened and Jax was thrust in so harshly that he stumbled and fell into Nicole. She caught him to her, helping him regain his balance.

"Jax?" she was surprised. "They caught you?"

He touched her cheek. In the darkness she noticed that his hand felt just right against her skin.

"More like we were betrayed. Jason works for Carlos."

Nicole felt as if she'd been kicked by a horse. She almost sat down but she forced her legs to hold steady. "Jason? Why?"

"He says it's the money."

"What are we going to do?" Nicole felt suddenly lost. All along she'd counted on Jax to come to the rescue. Now he was in as much trouble as she and her father.

So THE MASKS are all coming off, and the end result is that the A Team has been captured. Looks like I'm the only operative who hasn't been caught. Ah, the arrogance of the humanoid. They think I'm just a cat. Jason and Carlos Sanchez can't be bothered with me because I'm not worth the effort.

We'll just see about that.

I've memorized the telephone number that was on the scrap of paper in the parking lot. Vincent left that number, but I don't know why. I have two choices here. I can call the police, or I can dial that number.

My concern with the coppers is that if they come vaulting in here, Sanchez will kill Nicole, Jax and Vincent. On the other hand, that number may be another cohort of Sanchez and it might only bring in reinforcements.

I suppose I'll just do what I have to do.

Eeny, meeny, miny, mo! No, I'm not going to choose that way. I'm going to use my powerful feline brain. And the number I pick is the mysterious one.

Okay, here goes. I'm dialing from the telephone in Carlos's very well-appointed library. The line is ringing. It's one of those tinny rings, like calling to Europe.

There's a voice answering, and a voice I recognize. It's Monica Kane!

"Who is this? Who has this number! Tell me who this is!"

I'm going to give her a meow and see if she's smart enough to figure out how to trace the call. I'll leave the line open.

Now I'm putting on my best caterwauling voice and I hear her gasp of recognition. She knows it's me, and she knows something is up.

I only wish I knew which team she was playing on.

Uh-oh, here comes footsteps. Jason, that double-

dealing skunk, no doubt. I can't risk him finding the phone off the hook. I have to hang it back up and duck into a dark place. I don't think he's looking for me. I don't think he remembers I'm even here. Well, shoot that theory down. He's calling kitty, kitty. Like I'd fall for that.

He's saying he has poached salmon.

Man, that's tough. I sure could use a little sustenance right now. But I guess I'll have to wait. Somehow, I suspect the fish is laced with poison. I underestimated him though. He certainly went straight for my weakness—food.

JAX STOOD BETWEEN Nicole and her father, one arm lightly supporting Vincent and the other holding Nicole back as Carlos Sanchez stepped into the room.

"One thing I always admired about you, Vincent, is your ability to produce loyalty." Carlos and Jason stepped into the center of the room. Carlos talked and Jason held a semiautomatic pistol. "Your daughter is a fine example. She's been loyal for the past twenty years. Such a shame to see that turned in another direction. Now tell me where the diamond is."

"I don't have it." Vincent stood tall. "I never had it. I told you the truth."

"I'll say one thing for you, once you develop a story, you stick to it. But this isn't going to work. See, if you don't tell me where the diamond is, I'm going to hurt your daughter. Little by little, I'll make her wish she were dead."

Jax's fists clenched at his side. But Jason had a

gun and he had no weapon at all. He might be able to take Jason down, but he couldn't risk what might result. A stray bullet could kill Nicole or Vincent, or both.

"If I had the stone, I'd give it to you," Vincent said in a tired voice. "I never wanted it in my shop. I told Monica that I'd heard the stone was cursed. But she was determined to have it. She said it would bring out the lavender in her eyes. She convinced Richard Weeks to buy the stone from a dealer in Morocco. When that stone entered the premises of my shop, I knew that it was trouble. I should have followed my instincts and sent it right back out."

"Enough regrets," Carlos said, and there was a totally new tone to his voice. "Give me the stone and quit delaying."

Vincent glanced at Jax. They'd had only a few moments to try to make a plan. "You promise you won't hurt Nicole?" Vincent asked in a tone that held surrender.

"I only want the diamond," Carlos said, a grin of victory spreading over his face. "Only the diamond."

"Are you sure?" Vincent asked. "It's cursed."

"Only fools believe in superstition. No stone can be cursed. It's the power of the superstitious mind that creates mythology."

Vincent shrugged. "It's—"

He stopped as the sound of footsteps came toward them. Carlos froze and Jason swung the gun toward the door.

Jax saw his moment and leaped forward. His disciplined body hurtled through the air and he struck Jason in the solar plexus with his shoulder. It was a lucky hit, knocking the wind out of the other man.

The gun skittered across the floor and suddenly a black paw darted out from beneath the bed and snagged it, pulling it far out of reach.

Jax grinned. "Good work, Familiar," he called out as he pummeled Jason into submission.

Across the room he could see that Nicole had taken the opportunity presented to use a series of sidekicks on Carlos Sanchez. The lawyer had slammed into a wall and was now sitting on the floor, his hands held up to protect himself.

"Enough!" Jason cried out as Jax landed a sucker punch to his jaw. "Enough!"

Jax leaned down into Jason's ear. "I hope he paid you up front, because he's not going to have a chance to pay you now."

"Well, well, boys and girls," a feminine voice called from the doorway. "Look at all the fun we're having today."

"Monica!" Vincent called out, shock evident in his face. "How did you know to come here?"

"I got a phone call and I decided this was the perfect time to tidy up a few loose ends," she said, lifting the gun from her side and pointing it at Jax. "Get over by Vincent," she ordered. "Take Nicole with you. Carlos, I want you and your friend, there, to move over to this side of the room."

"Monica," Carlos said, catching his breath. "What are you doing here?"

"I heard that damn cat on the phone and I recognized your number on my caller ID. What I don't understand is how you talked Richard into sending me to the Brown Derby. I thought he was on to me," Monica said, an edge of nervousness in her voice.

Carlos dusted his hands. "It doesn't matter how you got here. I'm very glad to see you. I was about to convince Vincent to tell me where he's hidden the diamond."

"Oh, really," Monica said, her tone amused. "Why don't you tell us where you hid the diamond, Vincent? I'd really love to hear this."

Chapter Eighteen

Nicole took the position that Monica indicated beside Jax and her father. She let her gaze slip to the bed only once. Familiar was under the bed, with the gun. But what could he do? Even the smartest cat detective couldn't hold a semiautomatic and fire it.

"Monica, darling, I know how much you loved that diamond. It was the most spectacular jewel when you wore it." Carlos had obviously regained his confidence, though he continued to cast angry glances at the semiconscious Jason. "It's such a pity that once I recover it, it can't be worn in public. Perhaps we could have a private dinner. It would honor me if you wore the necklace again."

"Your generosity overwhelms me," Monica said.

There was something in her tone that made Nicole freeze. She glanced at her father and saw that he, too, heard it.

"You have the diamond, don't you, Monica?" Vincent said softly. "You've had it all along."

"Of course, darling," Monica said with a grin. "All of these years, I've put it on every night and let it warm me. It is the most exquisite stone in the world.''

Nicole saw total surprise register on Carlos's face. She glanced at Jax, who looked at Monica with horrified wonder.

''You let an innocent man stay in prison for twenty years?'' Jax asked her.

''Vincent wasn't innocent. No man is innocent. He was stupid, and his own stupidity tripped him up. He lied to protect me, and in doing so, he took the rap.'' Monica laughed.

''What's she talking about, Dad?'' Nicole asked him. ''You didn't lie, did you?''

Vincent took a deep breath. ''Only about one thing. I never told anyone that Monica knew the combination to the safe. I did it to protect her, because I couldn't believe she'd steal that diamond on the eve of her triumph in Hollywood.''

''Triumph? I knew I wouldn't win. I was never the darling of the town like some others. I had to fight for everything I ever got. I didn't stand a chance of getting an Oscar, but I also knew that it was the perfect opportunity for me to steal the diamond and never get caught.''

''While I was in prison, Monica visited me.'' Vincent spoke in a sad monotone. ''She promised that when I got out, she'd hire a private investigator to hunt for the diamond. She convinced me that she was on my side. That's why I left her phone number on that slip of paper. I thought if anyone could help you, Nicole, it would be Monica.''

"And I had it all along." Monica was almost gleeful.

"You threw everything away for a piece of rock?" Nicole asked, astounded.

"Don't act like such a child," Monica said harshly. "I had something real, the most magnificent diamond in the world. I've had it in my possession for twenty years. I had plenty."

"You threw two wonderful men away. You sent my father to prison for a crime he didn't commit." Nicole couldn't stop herself. She didn't have an inkling of what made Monica tick. "What about your career?"

"John's love for me made him weak. Richard's love made him possessive. I can't abide either trait. I only wanted to be rid of them. Love is a very transitory emotion."

"I don't believe that," Nicole said. Looking at the ugly twist that had become Monica's mouth, Nicole suddenly realized something about the woman who held the gun. "You changed, Monica. You turned into a monster and neither of those men wanted *you*. They couldn't stand what the diamond was doing to you and they walked away from you, just like the audience did. Everyone began to see what the diamond had turned you into—a greedy, grasping and very desperate woman."

"Shut up!" Monica leveled the gun at Nicole. "I understand why Angela Myers hates you so. You're a milksop and a do-gooder. But I won't have to be troubled with you for very long."

"Yes, I'm afraid we're going to have to get rid of them," Carlos said, starting toward Monica.

She swung the gun at him. "Not so quick, my legal friend," she said with a cold smile. "You're in as much trouble as they are."

"Monica, I'm just delighted to find the stone. After all these years, it'll be wonderful to see it out in public again."

"The stone belongs to Regency Insurance," Jax said. "I don't think Monica intends to go public with it. I don't think she wants to risk giving it back to the insurance company."

"But that's the benefit of having a good lawyer," Carlos said, easing even closer to Monica. "I was involved with the stone since it first came to this country. I handled the sale to Richard, the insurance policy, everything. And I did a brilliant job," he said, "because all along I knew it would end up in the hands of someone who loved and deserved it."

Monica laughed. "You thought it would end up in your hands, didn't you? This must be a crushing disappointment, Carlos. But let me just say that I wouldn't trust you to go to the corner and get me a newspaper. But you have given me some valuable information. I gather you wrote the policy on the stone so that you could legally obtain ownership of the diamond." She arched her eyebrows. "Thank you, Carlos. I appreciate all of your efforts."

"What are you going to do?" Carlos asked.

"Vincent and his daughter have to die. I knew when he got out of jail that he'd never stop hunting for the diamond. Eventually, he would have figured out that I had it.''

"I'm not so certain of that," Vincent said. "I don't know that I would ever have believed that you betrayed me, Monica.''

Monica ignored him. "I suppose Jax will have to die, too. He doesn't strike me as the kind of man who can be bought." She shook her dark hair. "Such a shame.''

Nicole put an arm around her father to steady him. Vincent was still weak, and the revelation that both Monica and his lawyer had betrayed him had struck him hard. She glanced at Jax and saw the anger in his eyes. But Monica held the gun, and she acted as if she knew how to use it.

"As for you, Carlos, I haven't decided what to do with you. But I think I'll have to kill you, too. See, if I can make it appear that Vincent had the diamond all along, and that the two of you fought over it, I can walk out of this smelling like a rose.''

Nicole saw that Monica was correct. She could have her cake and eat it, too.

"Monica, what happened to you?" Vincent asked softly. "When you first asked me about designing the jewels for you, you were the loveliest woman I'd ever seen. Part of that beauty was because of what was inside you. What happened?''

"She lost her dream," Jax said. "She lost who she was. The diamond is cursed.''

"Believe whatever makes it easier for you," Monica said, "but get ready to die.''

Nicole took a deep breath. She nodded at Jax. They had to rush Monica, no matter what else happened. She saw his answering nod and tightened her muscles to prepare to spring.

Before she could move a black shadow skittered out from under the bed. Familiar pushed the gun to Jax's feet and then took a flying leap through the air. He landed on Monica's chest with all four claws digging in. One large black paw reached up and raked down Monica's check.

Monica's scream filled the room, seeming to echo off the walls. She spun and slapped at the cat, but Familiar had a good hold, his claws digging deep into her skin. He held on as Monica whirled, finding every opportunity to claw her face.

Nicole seized the moment and threw herself at Monica's hips, bringing the actress down so hard she hit the floor with a whoosh and her gun went flying across the room.

Out of the corner of her eye, Nicole saw Jason start to make a grab for Monica's gun.

"Jason, I'll shoot you in the leg," Jax said calmly as he held the gun Familiar had deposited at his feet. He walked over and helped Nicole off Monica.

"My face! My face!" Monica sobbed as she looked at the blood dripping onto her hands.

"Before we do any talking, I think we should tie them up," Jax said with a slow grin. "It's a trick I learned in Texas. Before you go off bragging about what you're going to do, you'd better have the competition corralled."

"It'll be my pleasure," Nicole said as she went to the windows and pulled the cords from the draperies. She returned in a moment and quickly began the job of hog-tying Monica, Jason and Carlos.

"You give excellent directions," she told Jax when she had all three lying on their stomachs with feet tied to their hands. "I don't think they're going anywhere."

"Meow!" Familiar said. He walked to Carlos and climbed up on him. In a moment he was sitting on top of the prone lawyer. Familiar began grooming himself.

"Get that cat off me," Carlos said.

"I need a doctor," Monica said. "A plastic surgeon. My face! How bad is it?"

"What Familiar did to you is superficial," Nicole said. "And not nearly as bad as what I'd like to do to you."

"My face is my career," Monica said.

"Stop whining," Carlos ordered Monica. "This is all your fault."

"I want to see the diamond," Nicole told Jax. "I just want to look at a stone that's so valuable it's been worth all of this."

"I aim to oblige," Jax said, sauntering over to the corner where Monica and Carlos lay.

"Now, Monica, where's the diamond?" Jax asked as he knelt down and stared at her.

"Go to hell," she muttered.

"Wrong answer," Jax said.

"Familiar, I know how much Monica loves you.

Why don't you move camp over here?'' Jax suggested.

Familiar slipped off the lawyer and walked to Monica. He looked right into her face and yawned.

"Get that cat away from me," Monica said, acting as if she still commanded obedience from anyone who heard her.

"Familiar wants you to talk," Nicole said, joining in the fun with Jax. "Are your claws sharp enough?" she asked the cat.

Familiar quickly began digging his claws into the carpet, sharpening them.

"No! Don't let that cat near my face!" Monica said, her voice filled with desperation. "The diamond is in a safe in my house. It's behind the Monet."

"What's the combination?" Jax asked.

"Vincent knows it," Monica said bitterly. "It's the same combination that was on his safe."

"I know it well," Vincent said. "I think we should recover that diamond and turn it in to the police."

"A capital idea," Jax said. "Just one more detail here. I'm calling the cops."

As Jax started to punch in the three digits for an emergency, Nicole heard footsteps running toward them.

"The police are on the way!" Connie called out in a loud voice. "Nicole! Jax! Where are you?"

"We're in here," Jax called out to her. In a moment the young redhead was standing in the doorway, her eyes wide.

"You've already caught them," she said with pride. "They're all trussed and ready for delivery. Looks like rodeo night at Amarillo."

She walked over to Jason and nudged him with her foot. "You put something in my cola," she said with some heat. "You drugged me. But I didn't drink enough of it to stay out long. And just let me tell you that you are a low-down skunk and you're stupid to boot. You left his address on the pad by Nicole's telephone."

Connie turned to Monica. "What happened to your face? I heard Wes Craven was looking for someone to play a zombie in his next movie! You'll get the part hands down and they can save on makeup."

Connie's comments set off another series of complaints from the movie star.

"Now, will somebody tell me exactly what happened here?" Connie asked. "I'm sure Familiar played a big part in apprehending these criminals."

"It's all come full circle," Nicole said. She bent down and scooped Familiar into her arms. "This guy saved the day. But he had some exceptional help." She leaned over and kissed Jax on the lips. It was a taste of heaven, but she knew she could only have a taste. When she broke the kiss her father was looking at her.

"The cat is quite remarkable," Vincent said. "Can we keep him?"

"No, he has his own humans," Nicole said, kissing the top of Familiar's head. "They'd be heartbroken without him."

"Well, perhaps we can keep the other one," Vincent said, a sparkle in his eyes.

"The other what?" Nicole said. "There isn't another cat?"

"The other *one*. Him." Vincent pointed at Jax. "I rather like him, Nicole. I think we should keep him around on a permanent basis."

"Grand idea," Connie threw in.

"Dad! Connie!" Nicole couldn't believe it. They were only moments past potential death and her father was already trying to barter her into some kind of permanent relationship and Connie was ready to act as witness to the exchange.

"I'd very much like to be part of the family," Jax said, walking over and putting his arm possessively around Nicole. "Something permanent sounds terrific to me."

"Is that a proposal, young man?" Vincent asked.

"Dad!" Nicole wanted to pelt them both. They were acting as if they controlled her future.

"It's most certainly a proposal," Jax said.

Those words stopped Nicole short. She turned to Jax, Familiar still in her arms. "What?"

"He's asking you to marry him, Nicole."

She whirled and turned to her father. "Stay out of this, Dad. Please." She saw the hard lines in his face soften.

"You look just like your mother when she was annoyed by one of my many infractions of polite rules,'' he said. ''Why don't you two go outside? Connie and I'll stay here and guard the criminal element.''

''Dad, are you sure?'' Nicole asked as she watched her father take the gun from Jax.

''Honey, I'm a very good shot. Never saw the need to advertise it, but I can handle three hog-tied felons. You two go out and plan a wedding.''

''Yeah, do what your daddy tells you,'' Connie threw in with a big grin.

JAX HESITATED in the den, but it didn't feel right. Instead, he led Nicole outside. The back of the house was a magnificent garden. Tulips and daffodils were everywhere, and right in the middle of it all was a wooden bench. That was the perfect place.

He walked Nicole there and sat her down. He dropped to one knee and picked up her hand. ''Marry me, Nicole.''

''No pretty speeches or promises?'' she asked, her free hand going to his face.

''I promise that I'll love you for an eternity.''

''And what do you want me to promise?'' she asked.

''That you'll do the same. Can you do that?''

''With all of my heart. I'd love to be your wife,'' Nicole said, leaning down to gently kiss his lips. ''I never thought I'd fall in love with anyone,'' she said. ''And I never thought I'd be able to prove my father was innocent.''

"But you did," Jax said, his lips moving over her, demanding a deeper kiss.

"With your help," she said, her voice going lower.

He could feel the sudden hunger in her kiss. They'd gone from co-workers to being in love so fast they'd skipped a thousand steps.

"We haven't really had a first date," Jax reminded her.

"Or a second date."

"Or a first fight," Jax said, easing onto the bench beside her.

"Or a first night together," Nicole said breathlessly.

"Ah, that first night together. That's something I'm definitely looking forward to."

"Maybe we should get that out of the way tonight," Nicole said.

Jax pulled her into his arms and kissed her. It was a gentle kiss, but one that spoke of his hunger for her, his need. "I don't know if I can wait."

He felt her yield, surrendering to her own desire for him, and it was the most exciting sensation he'd ever known. Leaping from buildings and crashing cars, for all the adrenaline rush, was nothing compared to the feel of Nicole in his arms, awakening to her desire for him. He'd never known anything more exciting.

"We can go to a hotel," Nicole whispered.

"A wonderful idea," Jax said, almost devastated

by the mental images that danced in his head. "Just as soon as we tie up a few loose ends."

"The diamond? Should we actually touch it? I'm beginning to think it really may be cursed."

"It's eluded Vincent for twenty ears. I don't think we have to physically touch it, but I want to give the location to the authorities."

"Sounds like a plan," Nicole said, the fire of hunger still in her eyes, "and then you belong to me."

AH, YOUNG LOVE. I thought I was going to have to get the water hose and turn it on those two. But won't it be exciting to see another wedding?

I hear the wail of sirens. Thank goodness. I'll be glad to see Monica and Carlos behind bars. I've seen some dangerous characters before, but I think Monica Kane may be one of the most deadly. It's her beauty. She looks like an angel, but she doesn't have a heart. I think she's headed to prison for a long, long time.

Now, while the coppers are cleaning up the rat's nest, I think I'll scope out the kitchen. I am famished. Carlos Sanchez may be a skunk, but he's a wealthy skunk. That means he's going to have something really delicious in the fridge.

Chapter Nineteen

"And do you, Nicole, take this man to be your lawfully wedded husband?" the minister asked.

"I do," Nicole said, holding tightly to Jax's hand.

"I now pronounce you man and wife," the minister said. "You may kiss the bride."

Nicole felt Jax lift the veil, and then she was in his arms. There was no escaping the power of his kiss, and she closed her eyes and kissed him back. It didn't matter that she was wearing a wedding gown supplied by the costume person or that the wedding itself was on the set of a movie.

Far in the distance she could hear the whooping and hollering of the cast and crew. In celebration of their marriage, John Hudson had arranged for the caterer to bring in champagne, and she heard the sound of the first cork popping. John had magnanimously given everyone some time off.

"Hey, Jax," O. J. Adams called out. "Give the rest of us a chance to kiss the bride. It's tradition!"

"Not on your life," Jax said when he finally broke the kiss. His arms were still on Nicole, steadying her.

Nicole felt a little dizzy as she accepted the best wishes of all the cast and crew. Beside her, Connie stood as her maid of honor. Familiar, always attired in elegant black, had served as best man.

A few feet away, Vincent was in the center of a group of people, all asking him about the Dream of Isis and how it felt to be vindicated.

"Nicole, I'm sorry for all you've been through," John Hudson said as he came up to her. "I can't imagine how difficult all of this must have been. I feel badly that I didn't believe in Vincent more."

She could see the sadness in his eyes. Jax had been right; John still cared for Monica. Her betrayal of everyone had cut him as deeply as anyone else.

"It's over, John. That's what counts. I know Monica hurt you a lot, too. You and a lot of other people. But she's in jail now, and my father's name is cleared. He's starting his business again. He isn't that old. He still has plenty of time to design."

"Perhaps he'll get a chance to design for another Oscar nominee."

"I doubt that," Nicole said. "I don't think he's interested."

"But perhaps he would be if that nominee was his daughter." John's craggy eyebrows rose in anticipation.

"What are you talking about?"

"My next movie. I want you to star in it. I have the perfect script for you."

"But I'm a stuntwoman, not an actress."

"She's both," Jax said, stepping forward and kissing her cheek. "Take the risk, Nicole. You can do it. You'll be stupendous at it."

"Do it, Nicole. You'll be terrific." Connie was beaming with delight.

Nicole was stunned. She looked at the man who'd only moments before become her husband. "You knew about this, didn't you?"

His grin was his answer. "It's just another little wedding present I arranged for you."

John laughed out loud. "Just like you, Jax, to try and take all the credit. As charming as Mr. McClure is, he had nothing to do with my decision to offer you a movie role. What do you say, Nicole?"

"Okay," she said, feeling Jax's arm tighten around her. "I'll *read* for the part."

"Excellent. And Connie is going to be in it, too. A much bigger part than the last one. I think the two of you will shine together."

Connie's whoop of excitement made Nicole smile. Life had certainly turned around for her and everyone she cared about. She couldn't help but wonder if it was because the diamond was finally out of her life. The authorities had recovered it from Monica's safe and it would be returned to its rightful owner.

John strolled off, and for a moment, Nicole was alone with her new husband. Three weeks of a honeymoon stretched before them. Jax had arranged for a romantic trip to Tahiti, and she was more than ready to go.

She saw Peter and Eleanor Curry, Familiar's humans, and she slipped away from Jax and went to them.

"If you ever need a home for Familiar," she said, knowing that the black cat would never lack for love, "I'm available."

"As much as he worries us," Eleanor said, "we can't imagine life without him. I only hope he hasn't been bitten by the movie bug. He does have something of an ego, you know."

"Meow!"

Familiar had come up beside Nicole and she scooped him into her arms. "He saved our lives."

"Oh, please," Peter said. "His head is big enough."

"Me-ow!" Familiar took a swipe at Peter.

"He's a very special cat," Nicole said, putting him on his feet.

"And you must be a very special person for Familiar to get involved in helping you," Eleanor said. "And a lovely bride. We wish you both all the happiness."

"If I had one drop more, I think I'd die," Nicole said as Jax came up beside her.

"It's tradition for the bride and groom to have the first dance," Jax said to her. "May I?"

"This dance, and every dance for the rest of our lives," Nicole said as she was swept against his strong chest and into the rhythm of the music.

THE HUMANOIDS are participating in the dancing ritual, and that's good. Now I'm going to sample the buffet and indulge in a few delicacies.

The movie will wrap tomorrow, and then who knows what new adventures lie ahead for Familiar, black cat detective and sleuth into the dark mysteries of the human heart.

All I can say is that as much as I've enjoyed my trip to Tinsel town, I'll be glad to get home to Washington, D.C., and the ever elegant Clotilde!

HARLEQUIN®
INTRIGUE®

has a new lineup of books to keep you on the edge of your seat throughout the winter. So be on the alert for...

BACHELORS AT LARGE

Bold and brash—these men have sworn to serve and protect as officers of the law...and only the most special women can "catch" these good guys!

UNDER HIS PROTECTION
BY AMY J. FETZER
(October 2003)

UNMARKED MAN
BY DARLENE SCALERA
(November 2003)

BOYS IN BLUE
A special 3-in-1 volume with
REBECCA YORK (Ruth Glick writing as Rebecca York),
ANN VOSS PETERSON AND PATRICIA ROSEMOOR
(December 2003)

CONCEALED WEAPON
BY SUSAN PETERSON
(January 2004)

GUARDIAN OF HER HEART
BY LINDA O. JOHNSTON
(February 2004)

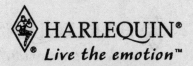

HARLEQUIN®
® *Live the emotion*™

**Visit us at www.eHarlequin.com
and www.tryintrigue.com**

HIBBONTS

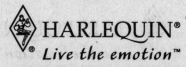

An offer you can't afford to refuse!

High-valued coupons for upcoming books

A sneak peek at Harlequin's newest line— Harlequin Flipside™

Send away for a hardcover by *New York Times* bestselling author Debbie Macomber

How can you get all this?

Buy four Harlequin or Silhouette books during October–December 2003, fill out the form below and send the form and four proofs of purchase (cash register receipts) to the address below.

I accept this amazing offer!
Send me a coupon booklet:

Name (PLEASE PRINT)

Address _____ Apt. #

City _____ State/Prov. _____ Zip/Postal Code
098 KIN DXHT

Please send this form, along with your cash register receipts
as proofs of purchase, to:

In the U.S.:
Harlequin Coupon Booklet Offer, P.O. Box 9071, Buffalo, NY 14269-9071

In Canada:
Harlequin Coupon Booklet Offer, P.O. Box 609, Fort Erie, Ontario L2A 5X3

Allow 4–6 weeks for delivery. Offer expires December 31, 2003.
Offer good only while quantities last.

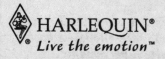

Visit us at www.eHarlequin.com

Q42003

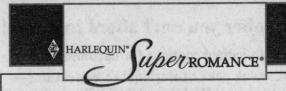

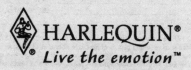

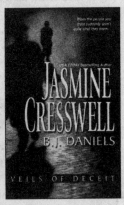